JACK SHIAN AND THE KING'S CHALICE

JACK SHIAN

AND THE
KING'S CHALICE

Book 1 in
The Shian Quest Trilogy

ANDREW SYMON

BLACK & WHITE PUBLISHING

First published 2013
by Black & White Publishing Ltd
29 Ocean Drive, Edinburgh EH6 6JL

1 3 5 7 9 10 8 6 4 2   13 14 15 16

ISBN: 978 1 84502 553 3

Back cover illustrations by Rossi Gifford.

A CIP catalogue record for this book is available
from the British Library.

ALBA | CHRUTHACHAIL

Typeset by RefineCatch Ltd, Bungay, Suffolk
Printed and bound by Nørhaven A/S, Denmark

To Maggie

Acknowledgements

I'd like to thank Ian Black for all his support and advice in getting this far. Slàinte!

CONTENTS

Shian (pronounced Shee-an [ʃiː + iən]):

n, the otherworld; creatures living in or coming from the otherworld. Also called daemons, fey, gentry, *daoine matha* [*good men*], portunes, etc. (C. 14; origins debated)

www.shianquest.com

Prologue

When Jack Shian was twelve, he was just growing into his magycks.

The Shian had always had magycks. Some had a little, some a little more. Charms, hexes, healing – all sorts. The magycks became much stronger when the Destiny Stone came home – it even opened up the Shian square under Edinburgh castle once more. Little wonder that the Shian celebrated; the Stone had been gone for hundreds of years, you see. That's hundreds of years in human time *and* Shian time; they're not always the same.

Shian can look like any creature you've ever imagined, and many that you haven't. Most humans have forgotten about the Shian, even the ones that look like humans, but they've always been there.

The Shian square opening up again meant that families were moving into the old houses, and craftsmen were getting the workshops going again. The craftsmen were employing apprentices too – that's the Shian way. A youngster who has 'grown into the magycks' is of an age to become an apprentice.

When the Shian Congress allocated Jack to work with Gilmore the tailor, it was decided that the whole family would settle in the Shian square, and so Jack *and* his aunt *and* his younger cousins moved from the quiet glen of Rangie just south of Edinburgh to join his older cousin Petros and Uncle Doonya in the Shian square. Jack's mum and dad aren't around at the moment because ... well, you'll find out why.

When Jack Shian was twelve and he was just growing into his magycks, everything changed.

1
Hobshee Hooligans

Screams startled Jack out of his daydream. He realised he couldn't see his uncle or Petros, but he *could* see that the girls were terrified.

"What's happening?"

"Over there." Rana, pale with fright, was pointing to a group of creatures about fifty yards away.

Even by Shian standards they were small – certainly smaller than Jack – but their obvious menace more than made up for any lack of height. Like a small platoon they moved swiftly across Falabray field towards the festival's main stage. Jack counted about a dozen of these creatures, as they upturned stalls and shoved others roughly aside. Then four broke away from the main group and set to work on demolishing two stalls, cackling and screeching with evident delight.

A stallholder moved forward, brandishing his sceptre. In a flash, one of the thuggish creatures had hurled a small stone at his feet. There was an explosion, and the stallholder fell, clutching his ears and screaming. His friends shrank back.

Jack's heart was drumming. He realised he had no idea who these creatures were.

"Where's Petros?" gasped Aunt Katie, arriving almost out of breath.

"He's with Grandpa," sobbed Lizzie. "Who—who're they?"

"The Hobshee; they're vandalising the festival."

"Enough!"

Atholmor's commanding voice had the desired effect. The Hobshee group halted ten yards from the central stage – from looking self-assured, they suddenly seemed unsure what to do. They hesitated, avoiding the Congress president's gaze.

"Who has brought you here?" roared Atholmor, holding his sceptre over the crowd.

None of the Hobshee seemed inclined to reply. Gnarled, grimy halflings, they squinted uncertainly up at the stage. Atholmor's fierce stare shifted to the northern edge of Falabray as a group of about twenty men and women on horseback appeared, their green cloaks flickering in the late evening light. They approached the central stage without sound or acknowledgement, unsmiling, stern of feature. Except for one rider, whose hood covered his face. Nausea swept through Jack.

He looks like the one who attacked me in the High Street!

"It's Briannan," said Grandpa Sandy, indicating the lead rider. He and Petros had silently joined the rest of the group. "I see he's brought his shock troops along."

The one called Briannan now reached the stage where Atholmor continued to stand commandingly.

"We have arrived," said Briannan in a drawling voice that demonstrated no warmth, "to join the festival. I am sorry if our diminutive friends have been a little ... exuberant." He smiled condescendingly.

Atholmor continued to hold his sceptre in front of him.

"Your 'friends' are not welcome here," he said in a low, steady voice. "On this most important festival they have desecrated this site. How do you account for them?"

"All Shian families are entitled to attend the midsummer festival," said Briannan firmly. "Our Hobshee friends cannot be disallowed on that front."

"They may be permitted, but their behaviour makes them most unwelcome." Atholmor chose each word with care.

"It is always pleasant to visit the festival and meet old ... friends." Briannan continued to scan the crowd, his voice showing no hint of emotion. Apart from that briefest of smiles, his face had been impassive. Now he turned to look up at Atholmor on the stage above him.

"Of course, if you wish to dismiss us from the festival you may do so. But I warn you that such an action will be long remembered. The Destiny Stone has not brought the power you believed it would."

Briannan made no attempt to hide the menace of these words.

"The Stone brings power to all Shian ..." began Atholmor.

"It brings *you* power, you mean," retorted Briannan. "But to work properly, it needs the other Shian treasures."

Atholmor paused. His shoulders seemed to sink slightly, but his gaze remained firm.

"The other treasures are lost – if they ever existed."

The side of Briannan's mouth twitched: half smile, half sneer.

"That stallholder . . ." began Atholmor.

"A harmless stun hex. He'll be fine."

Atholmor considered this for a few moments. "Then you are free to join in the festival," he said evenly. "But you would be well advised to keep your little army under control."

Satisfied with his moral victory, Briannan wheeled his horse around and started to trot off towards the north end of the field. Jack could see that there were three or four youngsters in addition to the men and women on horseback. One of them, a lad about his age with jet-black hair, looked over his shoulder contemptuously.

The air seemed somehow . . . tainted.

"It's time we were going," said Grandpa firmly, after ten minutes of growing tension. "Come along, young Jack. The rest of you too."

"Grandpa, who were those Shian?" Petros broke the silence as they passed through the bell hex, rising up to human size once more. "I didn't recognise any of them."

The bell hex had stopped any inquisitive humans from venturing up to Falabray, but now they were back in the human spaces and needed to be able to get about without attracting attention.

"That was the Brashat and their hired thugs, the Hobshee," said Grandpa. "I suppose we should have realised they would show up, but everyone was so excited about the festival, they didn't enter into our thoughts that much."

Jack toyed with the idea of mentioning the hooded figure, but decided against it. *They'll just tell me I'm imagining things.*

"Who are the Brashat?" he asked.

"That's a long story," said his grandfather. "They think they're the greatest Shian, because they rarely mix with humans. They also live much longer than we do, and that makes them look down on us."

"If they're not from round here," said Petros, "they wouldn't get any benefit from the Stone, would they?"

"That's true. Even so, I never thought they'd disrupt the festival. Briannan's a nasty piece of work, but he's manageable. I'm just glad Amadan the demon wasn't there. It was bad enough that they brought their little band of hooligans."

"Why did Atholmor let them stay, then?"

"Stun hexes don't last long. If they'd killed someone, that would've been different."

Jack realised he couldn't see his uncle. He turned to Petros.

"Where's your dad? I thought he was coming back with us."

"Doonya has stayed behind," replied Grandpa wearily. "He and the senior Congress will want to discuss tonight's little storm. I fear, too, there may be more storms ahead."

"I thought the Congress was organising everything, Grandpa," said Petros. "I mean, they're in charge, aren't they? How come they got it so wrong?"

Jack looked daggers at his big cousin, and decided to distract their grandfather. Pointing to a church clock, he asked, "A quarter past ten, Grandpa? How long were we up on Falabray?"

"Quite a while. It would have been longer if Briannan and his mob hadn't turned up. But down here for the humans it's only been a few minutes. You know the bell hex slowed time down, don't you?"

"Aye – Uncle Doonya told me."

Two fire engines raced past, their sirens blaring. Screeching to a halt outside a tenement building, several firefighters raced inside, dragging a coiled hose. Smoke billowed from an upstairs window.

"Cordita," said Grandpa. "I'd recognise that smell anywhere. The Brashat are up to their dirty work again, attacking humans. Come on, we'd better get back."

Edinburgh castle's esplanade was in dark shadow when they reached it. Grandpa and Petros motioned Jack to join them in forming a wall, behind which Aunt Katie, Rana and Lizzie crouched. Jack heard a brief *whishing* sound, and turning round saw that they had disappeared.

"You two next," said Grandpa, and Petros pulled Jack down so that they were squatting low behind their grandfather's cloak. Petros put his arm over Jack's shoulder, placed his left hand on the ground and whispered, "*Effatha!*"

Jack felt the increasingly familiar sensation of rapid movement, and moments later found himself standing in the Shian square across from the cottages. Aunt Katie brushed Lizzie's face as they walked towards their front door, while Rana protested about having to leave Falabray early.

"I'm sorry, Rana." Her mother tried to sound soothing, but the tremor in her voice betrayed her apprehension. "We didn't know the Hobshee would come and spoil things. There'll be other festivals."

"But the Seventh won't come around for ages, and we've been looking forward to it so much," wailed Rana, getting increasingly agitated. Lizzie's heavy sobs punctuated her sister's indignant complaint.

"Well, young Jack," said his grandfather, who had appeared beside him. "Tonight hasn't turned out quite the way we'd intended. But as we're back earlier than planned, perhaps we can after all visit the Stone tonight."

Jack's eyes lit up.

The Destiny Stone!

2
The Watchers of the Stone

Grandpa drew his cloak around Jack's shoulders and struck the ground firmly with his sceptre. Jack was briefly aware of a red glow, and moments later found himself in a small dimly-lit room. In the centre stood a large glass cabinet. Inside, Jack could just make out a crown, sword and sceptre ... but it was the object at the head of the cabinet that drew his attention. A large glistening sandstone block with an iron ring at either end.

The Stone, I've finally seen it.

Jack felt his pulse race as a warm feeling of joy swept through him.

"We're high up in the castle now," his grandfather said quietly, pointing his sceptre at the security cameras. "They'll be filming, but they won't see anything unusual. We can get a little light from this."

Grandpa waved his left arm in an arc and seven lit candles hovered beside them. He then clicked his fingers, and two armchairs appeared by the side of the glass cabinet.

"The Stone's only been back a few years. The humans think they know why it's important, but we need to go way back to understand why."

"I can feel it already, Grandpa. Like a pulsing, and my fingers are tingling."

"That's a good sign – you're tuned in. I'll show you something I've not long discovered. In truth, I got the idea from some humans. If I concentrate really hard, I can use my sceptre to project an image of what I'm thinking onto the wall. It's called a simulacrum."

Grandpa took a moment to gather his thoughts then aimed his sceptre at the wall. Jack watched in fascination as moving figures started to appear, indistinctly at first, as if moving through the mist, then much clearer.

The boy gripped his bow so hard that his knuckles pulsed.

As the soldiers emerged from the forest, they started to run, their swords drawn.

"Yeearrgh! Kill the Shian!"

The boy's heart thumped in his chest. These men wanted him dead. And not just him – everyone like him. Fear danced in his nostrils.

He fired.

"Not yet, son, save your flights. When they get closer – fire."

The soldiers charged closer . . . closer . . . One threw an axe, which embedded itself into the man next to him. The smell of fear now mingled with the smell of blood.

"Let them have it, son."

Twang! Twang!

Two soldiers fell, but more kept coming ... The boy could see the bulging eyes of the man nearest to him. The man swung a cleaver ...

Jack leapt back as the cleaver seemed to jump out of the simulacrum.

"Fierce battles, young Jack. Many died terrible deaths, or were tortured or burnt afterwards. The Brashat never forgave us for siding with the humans. It split the main Shian people into two: Seelie and Unseelie."

"Seelie?"

"The ones who mixed with humans. Those humans simply called us 'Shian', and for our family the name stuck. The Brashat were always scornful of us even having human names – said they couldn't tell us apart. These days, of course, hardly any Shian mix with humans. They keep to their world, and we keep to ours. As long as we're careful when we go out into the human spaces most of them don't even see us."

"Shian creatures too, Grandpa. Humans don't see them any more either, do they?"

"Not any more, but when humans built castles like this, you can tell they saw Shian creatures – just look at the carvings."

A hideous gargoyle peered out of the simulacrum at Jack.

"Way back, we even shared the Destiny Stone with the humans because it was important for both of us."

"Uncle Doonya told me that. He said the humans used it to crown kings."

"Ah, but it was the Shian who really knew what the Stone was. It absorbed energy from the local sandstone, but only gave this out to Shian. But with the Stone, our charms got much stronger. The clever humans could see that having powerful Shian allies was better than having powerful enemies."

"Shian and humans shouldn't mix!" shouted a disembodied face in the simulacrum.

"Hah," said Grandpa. "A Brashat. Well, it's true that some Shian hate the humans. Those house fires on the way back from Falabray were no accident."

Flames from a burning building flickered in the simulacrum. Jack could almost smell the cordita.

"So the Brashat use their power to destroy things?"

"Oh yes, and with the Stone's power, they'd be even worse. That's why the humans put iron rings on the Stone. If the wrong kind of Shian got it . . ."

"Everyone knows Shian can't go near iron," said Jack, staring at the rings. "But even with them the Stone's awesome. It gives off a . . . a kind of warmth."

"I know exactly what you mean," Grandpa smiled. "It *is* a warmth. It makes you feel good about yourself. You're a Watcher in the making, young Jack."

"Why did Briannan say the Stone hadn't brought the power we all thought it would?"

"Briannan is partly right," said Grandpa cautiously. "The Stone's return didn't change things straight away. But it was away for a long time; the energy may take years to flow at full strength. Some Shian groups – those ones who are furthest away from the Stone – are barely awake even now."

"But Briannan said the Stone needed other treasures to work properly."

"Oh, he was just making noises because the Brashat don't have the Stone."

"So the treasures don't even exist? Like Atholmor said?"

"They were just stories that ancient Shian told themselves when the Destiny Stone was far away."

"But what were the treasures?" persisted Jack.

Grandpa scratched his chin.

"I haven't heard anyone mention these since I was a boy. Let's see ..." His brow furrowed. "I remember one was an ancient silver cup – that's right, the French king's cup. The legends said it told secrets about life and death for Shian and humans, or something like that. But they're just stories."

Jack thought back to the festival and the Brashat leader's reaction when Atholmor had cast doubt on the treasures' existence – Briannan knew something! Jack was sure of it. But Grandpa obviously didn't believe this. Jack played for time.

"So we've just to wait for the Stone's energy to flow again?"

"It *is* flowing – the Shian square opening up after centuries is proof of that. And the force of the charms we can conjure up – like the bell hex we used at Falabray to keep the humans away – we couldn't do that while the Stone was away."

Jack looked at the grey sandstone block again. The corner nearest the crown had a bit missing – like it had been chipped – but Jack could feel it pulsing anyway.

"Just imagine having even that corner. That would be awesome!"

"Oh, there's no doubt it has power," continued his grand-father, watching Jack closely. "That's why Shian and humans have fought over it."

"Shouldn't all the Shian have joined together to have the Stone for ourselves?"

"There's many more humans than us, and they can do some things we can't, but the Watchers' pact benefited both sides. The Unseelie never accepted that deal."

"Arrrgh!" The Brashat in the simulacrum raged at historical injustices.

"Well, you've seen some of his sort tonight," said Grandpa. "And there's other Unseelie around the country. But as long as the Congress is in charge, they won't cause too much trouble. And now the Stone's back. Your father helped there – do you want to know more?"

Jack nodded.

"Then there's bits Uncle Doonya should tell you now."

Grandpa Sandy took up his sceptre and stood. Encasing Jack in his cloak, he struck the floor firmly with his sceptre. There was a rushing sense, which made Jack feel briefly giddy.

"I see Doonya has returned," said Grandpa, noting that the light was on in the front room of the house. "He can tell you about what happened next."

3
Family Secrets

"How did you get on with the Congress, then?" asked Grandpa, tapping the lumis crystals by the kitchen door and brightening the room.

Doonya's knuckles were drumming the tabletop, his edginess evident. Jack stayed by the door and watched him warily.

"To be upstaged by Briannan and his mob . . . Well, let's just say we should've seen it coming. It's given the Brashat something to crow about, but they can't do much unless they get someone here under the castle."

"I'll tell you something about that later. I've been telling young Jack about the Stone being returned. Now he'd like to know about his parents. Perhaps you'd pick up from there?"

Doonya looked quizzically at his father for a moment, then shrugged and motioned Jack to sit down.

"You were only tiny at the time, so I don't suppose you remember your dad helping us escort the Stone back," he began, "but he disappeared two nights after the Stone was placed in the castle."

"He can't have just disappeared." Jack could hear his voice betraying the upset he felt for a father he couldn't even remember. "Somebody must know where he is."

"D'you think we haven't looked?" snapped Doonya. Then more calmly, "He was seen talking with one of the Brashat lieutenants."

"But he wouldn't betray us to the Brashat!"

Grandpa held up his hand. "Calm down, young Jack." The soothing voice broke through Jack's fear. "We don't think he betrayed us. But the Brashat may have taken him, and they can count on other Shian who are no friends of ours."

"What kinds of Shian?" With a sickening feeling, Jack realised that his upbringing in Rangie had not prepared him for this.

"You've seen the Hobshee; they'll do what the Brashat tell them. Then there's blood-drinking Boaban Shee from the far north – a bit like vampires. And there's Red Caps – they dip their caps in their victims' blood."

Grandpa aimed his sceptre at the kitchen wall. As the simulacrum reformed, a grisly old man appeared, stooping over a fresh corpse. Clutching a bloody red cap, he looked up, leering into the kitchen. Jack felt the colour drain from his face.

"You never told me about Shian like that before," he whispered.

"There's Seelie and Unseelie all around the country," said Doonya. "That's why we need a strong Congress – to make sure the Unseelie don't unite."

"Amadan could unite them; I pray you never have to deal with him. We deliberately shielded you, that's why you've never left Rangie before. If your father was captured, whoever did it might have wanted to get you too – to put pressure on him."

"But why would they want to take him?"

"Your father told us he was on to something – something big that would make our family strong again. If the Brashat – or whoever – found out about that, well . . ."

The hooded figure who'd accosted him in the High Street flashed across Jack's mind. *Had he* really *been Shian? And had he really said 'father'?* The more Jack thought about it, the less sure he was.

"That's why my mother left, isn't it?" Jack played for time. "Aunt Katie told me that she left because she thought she'd be captured next."

"She *was* scared," said Doonya. "You never knew before, but a Brashat killed her own father. A stupid quarrel that got out of hand. She was never the same after that. And then when your dad disappeared, it just distracted her. All she could think of was evil Brashat coming to snatch her and Cleo. So she ran away."

"Why didn't she take me with her, then?" demanded Jack.

"Well, your mother was always quite . . . highly strung. Your dad's disappearance brought back memories of her own father's death. It was too much for her."

"What d'you mean, 'highly strung'?"

"After her father died, she became very . . . nervous. She felt she couldn't cope with you *and* Cleo."

A pause.

"She just didn't face problems well, young Jack. But you were better off in Rangie. The Brashat would never go there, it's too far away from their own places. They'd stand out."

"Then she would've been safe there too."

"She didn't see it that way. She panicked, and ran."

"She's had years to stop panicking, though," Jack shouted.

He felt numb. The explanations didn't convince. Maybe he just didn't want to hear them. For years he had been fobbed off with evasions and half-stories. But he'd always known there was something else, something no one wanted to tell him. And now the painful truth was upon him. His father had disappeared, possibly in an act of treachery, maybe kidnapped; his mother had run away, too scared to stay and look after him. He had a younger sister who might not even know of his existence.

One thing Jack knew: no one had ever felt this sense of betrayal. His uncle and aunt had always taught him to be proud of his family, but this was a lie – his parents had not protected or raised him. Unable to think of any other response, Jack jumped to his feet.

"It's a lie!" He thumped the table. "He didn't betray us!"

Storming out of the kitchen, he slammed the door and ran upstairs.

Grandpa Sandy stood up and exhaled slowly. "We might have handled that a bit better."

Jack slept late. When he awoke, he could hear his cousins downstairs as they clattered around the kitchen. Jack dreaded the thought of facing his uncle and grandfather. He decided to stay in bed for a while.

Gradually, the noise of his cousins and the smell of breakfast became too much for him. Dressing quickly, he slipped down to the kitchen, where Petros was at the sideboard, making toast on the open fire.

"You know the humans can make toast, perfectly brown on both sides?" he announced to his sisters. "I've seen the machine in the shops."

"Hi, Jack," called Rana, her face beaming. "That was exciting yesterday, wasn't it? I wasn't really scared. Dad would've sorted out those Brashat if they'd tried anything funny."

"There's hawberry pancakes here. Help yourself." Petros shoved a plate over.

"Was it exciting up at the Stone last night?" asked Lizzie.

"It was great," replied Jack, warming to the conversation. "I got a really strange feeling from it, sort of warm and fuzzy. Have you felt that too?"

"Sort of," replied Lizzie slowly. "I've only been there once. It doesn't look like much, does it?"

"Dad says it might not be the real Stone," pouted Rana. "There's a story that the real Stone was hidden, and this one's a fake."

"Yes, but this Stone's working, isn't it?" said Petros, his mouth full of toast. "It couldn't if it wasn't the real Stone."

"I think it's the real one," said Jack calmly, remembering the feeling he'd had sitting next to the Stone. "Grandpa says it's working because it's close to other sandstone. And Shian charms are working better again – even hexes."

"Look, Jack, Mum bought us a squillo." Lizzie reached into her skirt pocket and gently pulled out a small rodent. "Isn't he sweet!" she cooed, and despite himself, Jack began to smile.

"We'll call him Nuxie," announced Rana, leaning over and stroking the timid creature. "Let's take him out to the High Street," announced Rana. "Who wants to come?"

"You're getting used to the human spaces now, aren't you, Jack?" asked Petros. "D'you remember your first time?"

Of course I remember it, thought Jack. *It was only a few days ago!*

4
Midsummer

"Effatha!"

The Shian gate sprang open. Jack and Petros trebled in size as they emerged onto Edinburgh castle's sunlit esplanade. Jack felt his stomach lurch upwards – he still wasn't used to moving between the Shian and human spaces, but he concealed his queasiness from his cousin. If Petros saw that, he wouldn't take Jack beyond the esplanade.

The pair moved briskly down towards the Royal Mile, whose ancient smoke-blackened buildings loomed high in front of them. Wide-eyed, Jack looked around him at the baffling mixture of old and new, foreign and local.

"Quick, this way!" Petros urged, dragging Jack by the arm.

They both broke into a run, heading away from the castle.

"What's up?" panted Jack as he tried to keep pace.

"Over there," hissed Petros, pointing at a small crowd gathered near St Giles' Cathedral.

"Is it the juggler?"

Petros grimaced, and pointed at the far side of the crowd. A tall figure was slowly edging his way forwards. Inconspicuously dressed, he was nevertheless striking. Jack became aware of the muscles beside his eyes twitching. He'd had this feeling several times when out in the human parts of Edinburgh.

"He's Shian," whispered Petros. "Can't you tell?"

The tall figure glanced across at the two youngsters. There was a flicker of a smile, and an almost imperceptible nod.

"Oh, right." Jack grinned, feeling a bit safer. It was good to know they weren't the only Shian in this crowd. Humans were all right, but they were a bit . . . jostly.

The juggler, who had been busy setting fire to the end of five wooden staves, now addressed his audience in a loud and imperious voice.

"Ladies and gentlemen, Jongo the greatest juggler in the northern hemisphere – that's me, in case you were wondering," he gave a cheesy smile to the audience, "requires the help of a glamorous assistant."

A plump young woman stepped forward. Jongo regarded her briefly before looking round at the crowd and hissing in a stage whisper, "Not really glamorous enough."

The woman turned scarlet, and hurried away, her eyes downcast.

Some of the onlookers started muttering.

"There was no need for that . . ."

"Poor soul . . ."

Jongo gulped hard, realising he'd overstepped the mark, and was grateful when the tall stranger distracted the crowd's attention by stepping forward. The stranger stared hard at

Jongo for a moment. Unable to hold his gaze, Jongo addressed the crowd in general.

"Ah, a volunteer!" he cried extravagantly. "And where, sir, do you come from?"

The figure did not speak, but mimed 'far away' with a wave of his arm.

"A visitor to this cold city, sir, so am I. Now, lie down there!"

Jongo was back on form, and with an imperious wave, he pointed to a grubby mat. In a barking voice, he then explained to the crowd how he would juggle and throw the flaming staves towards the mat, but catch them before they landed and burned the volunteer to a crisp, a feat nobody else this side of the equator could match.

Jongo grasped all five staves and began to juggle, deliberately (or was it?) fumbling one or two. Some of the crowd started laughing, and others began to clap. At last, Jongo launched the staves into the air, but before he could complete the trick, the recumbent body burst into flames. The surprised performer stumbled and fell, looking on aghast as the figure before him was enveloped in fire. Gasping in horror, the crowd stepped back.

And then the figure stood up. The flames fell off him, and he dusted himself down as if nothing had happened. The crowd, overawed, did not know what to make of this. Then someone started to clap, and others joined in. Soon they were cheering delightedly and stamping their feet in approval. Jongo seized the opportunity and milked the applause, while glancing ruefully at the remains of the smouldering staves.

The tall figure melted back into the crowd and disappeared.

"Come on," said Petros. "That was cool, eh?"

Jack seemed frozen to the spot. Like the rest of the crowd, he was still trying to put a name to what he'd just seen. Then his eyes sparkled.

"A flame spirit!" he said, his face beaming. "I've never seen one before. That was brilliant."

"I bet he's here for the festival," said Petros. "I can't wait to tell Rana and Lizzie."

The festival! Jack's mind raced at the thought of the entertainment to come – just two days away now.

"I'm going to buy some floating charm stones too, and hexes that make humans forget who they are. Some of them are so stupid."

Petros laughed as he steered Jack back up the road. At thirteen, Petros was a year older than Jack, and had started his apprenticeship under the castle the previous summer.

"Come and see this," Petros announced, doubling back down the street and darting across the road.

Another shop full of human gadgets, moaned Jack inwardly. *Petros can't get enough of them*. Jack slowly began to cross the road to join Petros, who was gazing at a window display of cameras.

"Oww!"

An ice-cold hand grabbed Jack's shoulder roughly, its jaggy fingernails tearing through his shirt and drawing blood. Gasping in surprise and pain, Jack spun round. A man wearing a grubby hooded top, ill-fitting trousers and battered trainers snarled incomprehensibly. The hood up, Jack could barely see the man's face. He was muttering, the words were indistinct . . .

Did he say 'father'?

. . . but the tone was undoubtedly threatening. The muscles beside Jack's eyes started twitching furiously, and yet this produced a mixed response.

He's Shian. He's like me.

But at the same time, a feeling of dread filled Jack, and he felt sick. Releasing Jack, the man swept the hood off his head, revealing a hideously scarred face, and he mumbled something that was unmistakably angry. Jack's instinct was to run, and when the man made to grab him again, this cleared his mind: *Get out of here!*

He ducked away, and began to run up the street, only slowing down as he neared the castle esplanade. Gasping for breath, he stopped beside the warhorse memorial, hands resting on his knees. From here he could get a good view of everyone approaching the castle.

Jack's breathing slowly settled, and the sick feeling in the pit of his stomach eased a bit.

Why'd he try to grab me? And what about my father?

It was exactly one week since Jack had moved to his new home under the castle. One extraordinary week – the longest of his life.

Since arriving from Rangie with Rana and Lizzie, Jack hadn't ventured further than the castle and the esplanade. The High Street could wait, said Petros, and indeed it had, until today. (Jack had quickly learned to copy Petros's term, the 'High Street'. Only tourists call it the Royal Mile, Petros had said. Petros the city boy.) Uncle Doonya had agreed with Petros, explaining that Jack shouldn't cram too much in to the first few days. 'Sensory overload', he'd called it – a phrase that meant little to Jack. In the sheltered Shian glen of

Rangie, little changed from one month or one year to the next.

Now Jack had to get used to living in the Shian square, away from Rangie's woods and streams. He had to learn the charms that would get him into and out of the square without attracting attention, and he had to get used to being stretched up to full human height when out in the human spaces. This, he knew, was the secret of blending into his new surroundings. Relieved, he saw Petros jogging towards him.

"Where'd you get to?" gasped Petros. "I only went to look at some cameras. You shouldn't run off like that. 'Specially not on your first proper outing."

"S–Someone tried to grab me."

"Who?"

"I don't know who. He was Shian, that's all I know."

"What'd he look like?"

Jack described the man, his scarred face, his clothes and the way he'd behaved.

"That's just an old tramp," laughed Petros. "He was probably just after some money."

"But I'm sure he was Shian," persisted Jack.

"You just got confused by the shock," replied Petros. "It takes time to learn how to tell who's Shian in a crowd. Let's get back inside. Better not tell Mum or Dad, though. They'll only worry."

Approaching the castle gate, Petros deftly steered Jack past the guides. A few yards on, he turned and blew softly, whispering, "*Nubilus!*" A miniature cloud floated above a tourist group and began to discharge tiny raindrops. As tickets and guidebooks became wet, those holding them looked around, perplexed at the appearance of rain on a sunny evening.

A girl of about six or seven was looking on curiously. Seeing this, Petros winked at her. Then, chuckling to himself, he pulled Jack by the arm through the castle gate.

5
Edinburgh Castle

As they walked in silence up to the ramparts of Edinburgh Castle, Petros took a sly peek at his younger cousin. Although Shian people could usually pass as human, Petros prided himself he could spot the difference straight away. He noted that Jack's ears, sticking out from under a dark thatch of hair, were slightly pointed, and the short dark eyebrows – these gave Jack away instantly. *But humans don't notice things like that*, thought Petros. Enlarged up to human height like this, Jack wouldn't get a second glance from most humans – unless they looked him in the eyes. Then they couldn't miss it. Not just the piercing eyes – most Shian people had that – but the different colours: the dazzling light blue one on the right, set against the nut-brown eye on the left. A look that makes some humans feel uncomfortable.

"Come on," said Petros, "let's go up to the chapel. The view's really cool."

Petros carried his extra height with the self-assurance of one who knows the ropes. Having moved to the Shian square the previous year to start his own apprenticeship, he was now learning how to do *real* Shian things, like use charm stones, and even – unofficially – hexes. He enjoyed this position of seniority, but longed for Jack to settle in. They would have a lot more fun when Jack was less startled by everything, less nervous. *But he's always been a bit like that*, thought Petros. *I guess not remembering your parents can do that to you.*

They reached the parapet that stood high over the city, where the view looked over the majestic streets of Edinburgh's New Town and beyond to the river and the hills of Fife.

"How can so many people be in one place?" gasped Jack.

"There's half a million humans in Edinburgh." Petros idly kicked a stone. "More in the summertime. Visitors come from all over the world."

"But why?"

"There's different things to see here. Edinburgh's famous. People want to see the castle, and the city's cool too – there's loads to do."

The small girl had caught up with Jack and Petros, her curiosity awakened. Darting back now, she tugged on her mother's sleeve, demanding her attention.

"Come on." Petros pulled Jack towards the small chapel that stood nearby. "Grandpa said he'd meet us in the house. The castle closes soon. They lock the gates once they've got all the visitors out."

Or at least the gates they know about, he thought with a wry smile as he and Jack walked to where the chapel's west wall was embedded in rock. Petros looked carefully both ways. The small girl had followed them, watching inquisitively. *Oh well*, thought Petros. *Now she'll really have something to tell her mum.* He nodded to Jack, and they both leant forwards against the rock, closing their eyes. Petros put his right arm around Jack's shoulder, held up his left hand against the rock and whispered, "*Effatha!*"

Petros felt Jack tense up as they experienced the sensation of freefall movement. Seconds later they were at the side of the Shian square under the castle rock. Petros grinned as he saw Jack open his eyes.

"It's a good feeling, isn't it?"

"Ye . . . es," said Jack cautiously. "It . . . it's weird, like you're falling a long way very quickly. It still makes my guts feel funny." He turned his face gratefully towards the cool breeze that came from the warren pipes in the rock wall.

Just then two girls ran out of one of the houses opposite, laughing and pulling at a short wire.

"Petros, Jack, come and see what we've found," they said in unison.

"What is it?" asked Jack, intrigued by his young cousins' enthusiasm.

"Dad says it's a music box," said Rana.

"Somebody left it near the chapel," interrupted Lizzie.

"Oh, cool." Petros reached over and took the box, which – as he and Jack had done a moment earlier – had shrunk on passing through the Shian gate.

The twins were a year younger than Jack. While Petros had inherited his father's dark hair and looks, the twins (said everyone) resembled their mother, sharing as they did the same shock of strawberry blonde hair as her. Lizzie wore her hair long, but Rana, much to her mother's dismay, had long insisted on a short cut. Both had a love of 'finding' objects left behind by forgetful humans.

"You put these things in your ears, and you hear music." Lizzie tugged the small box away from her brother. "Look, I'll show you."

She took the two wires and put a small round white lump in each of Jack's ears. Rana pressed a button on the small box, and a far away sound of strange music came to him.

"I've heard music like that before," he said, after a few moments. "Back in Rangie. There were some human boys playing in the woods, and they had a music box. It was bigger than this, though, and the sound came out of the box, not wires like these." The white lumps were uncomfortable in his ears, and he pulled them out.

"It's not as good as a songstone," said Jack. "They play every tune you know, clearer than that, too. I'm going to save up and get one."

"We saw a flame spirit in the High Street," Petros informed his sisters as he took the gadget from Jack. "He played this really neat trick on a street juggler. You should've seen the juggler's face when the spirit burst into flames."

"Is he going to be at the festival?" asked Lizzie, wide-eyed.

"Sure," said Petros nonchalantly. "There'll be Shian from all over the place. Phooka, elves – you name it. Hoodwinks, too."

Their mother's voice echoed across the square. "There you are! Come along."

With a shrug, Petros led the others across the square.

"So, Jack dear, how did you find being up at the castle?" Aunt Katie ruffled Jack's hair as he sat down in the kitchen.

"The buses and cars are really loud. The houses below the castle looked tiny, but I know they're big really. I . . . I wanted . . ." Jack felt his heart racing.

"You're wondering about the Stone, aren't you?" She smiled at him. "Well, here's Grandpa now, you can ask him yourself."

"Jack wants to ask you about the Stone," said Petros, as the imposing figure of Grandpa Sandy appeared in the doorway. "He wanted to go up and see it today, but I said he'd have to wait and ask you and Dad."

"I . . . I wanted to see what it was like," began Jack. "Uncle Doonya's told me so many tales about it, I wanted to see it."

"And you will, very soon, young Jack. Maybe tomorrow."

It's always 'tomorrow', thought Jack.

"But we're going to be busy. There's lots to do to prepare for the festival." A broad smile spread across his grandfather's face.

Jack's disappointment faded. The midsummer festival was the high point of the Shian year, and the Stone's return had revived the ancient tradition of the Shian Seventh – a special countrywide celebration every seven years that brought Shian groups and families from all over for a huge carnival. And, best of all, in just two days it would be held on the Shian field below the great volcanic outcrop of Arthur's Seat.

6
The Shian Seventh

The next two days were frenetic. Grandpa and Uncle Doonya were constantly occupied with Shian Congress meetings, but Jack was kept so busy with household chores by Aunt Katie that he didn't have much time to think about going to see the Stone. In truth, he was relieved when evening came and it was finally time to leave for the festival.

The walk through the Edinburgh streets had taken only twenty minutes, but the climb up the slopes of Arthur's Seat was taking ages. Jack began to sweat. As they rounded a break in the rocks, a strange feeling of stillness came over him, and his stomach turned. Suddenly, he could hear the sound of a great crowd.

"We're through the bell hex and back to normal size," said Grandpa with a smile. "It's a special hex that keeps humans out. For some reason, none of them will have the slightest inclination to climb up here tonight." He winked at Jack.

"Did you see the flame spirits?" Lizzie's eyes sparkled as she ran back to join the family. "I saw one do this amazing trick. She floated up and breathed on this barrel, and it melted and out came two goats."

Uncle Doonya laughed. "Well, you know that a lot of Shian can change their shape when they want."

A stooping figure walked up and faced Grandpa.

"It's good to see you, Sandy," he said calmly.

"Rowan! Everybody, this is Rowan, he's been working for the Congress in the low countries since the last Seventh, and now he's been asked to join the Congress. It's good to see you again, my friend."

Jack sensed real warmth in Grandpa's voice as the two old men embraced.

"I'm so honoured to have been asked. It's been a privilege to work for the Congress for so long, but to join the most important Shian group in the country . . ." Rowan wiped a tear away.

"Well, I'm delighted for you, my old friend." Turning to the others Grandpa added, "Rowan was in the procession seven years ago."

"You'll be Phineas's young boy," said Rowan, turning to Jack, and smiling.

"That . . . that's right."

"Looking to get some of the Stone's power, eh?" chuckled Rowan.

Jack looked up enquiringly at his grandfather.

"The Stone's power is for all Shian," smiled Grandpa. "Now, here comes the procession."

Jack turned to watch as fourteen white horses appeared. Three pairs of men and women were followed by pairs of elves, dwarves, Darrigs and lastly two korrigans, who seemed miniscule even astride their tiny Shian ponies. The sound of distant trumpets soared on the still air, a high haunting sound.

The horses moved effortlessly, almost floating, and the huge crowd parted before them. Atholmor and his wife Samara led, quietly smiling and waving occasionally at a familiar face. As they approached the central stage, a high, constant trumpet note filled the air, louder and more insistent. The procession halted, and the trumpet stopped. Dismounting, Atholmor climbed up onto the wide stage.

"Friends," he said in a steady and commanding voice, "welcome to the Shian Seventh. I thank you all for coming. After many years, the Stone is close by once again, and many are recovering their ancient gifts. Let us rejoice in the return of the Stone! Let us celebrate the great Shian!"

"Here," said Petros as they wandered through the stalls. "We've a gold sovereign each. What d'you fancy?"

"Try these elven biscuits," said Rana. "They've got juniper jam in them."

"The silverweed cakes are fabulous," said Petros. Turning to Jack he added, "Silverweed only flowers every few years."

Jack, his mouth already full of pie, didn't reply.

"Dad, can I try some heather mead?" asked Petros.

"All right, a small cup, as it's a special night. You too, Jack, if you want to try it."

Soon after, they were watching three Icelandic elves reciting an epic, a long story that mixed the Destiny Stone in with an ancient chalice and a mystical globe. In turns they would act the part of various characters, their high croaky voices carrying a strange sense of mystery and urgency about the power of these three great treasures.

"They're funny," said Lizzie. "I've never met anyone from Iceland before. Are they all that small?"

"They come in all sizes," replied her father. "They tell human stories as well as their own."

"We read human stories, Dad," pointed out Rana. "We've been learning for ages. Mum's been teaching us."

"There's more of them up there too," continued her father patiently. "They're closer to the humans, they have more dealings with them."

Jack turned to speak to Uncle Doonya, but his eye was caught by the bright Edinburgh skyline behind them. His uncle saw the quizzical look in his eyes and whispered, "Time stands still, Jack my boy. This is midsummer – our time."

"You mean we can slow down time?"

"Only at certain times. Luckily for us, this is one of them," replied Doonya with satisfaction. "Didn't you feel something funny when you passed through the bell hex?"

Jack thought back to their ascent to Falabray field. He *had* felt something strange as they'd got close, but had put this down to shrinking back to Shian size again.

"Ah, here's Grandpa; he's good at explaining things."

"Actually, I wanted to take the youngsters to see the Phooka."

Grandpa led Jack and his cousins towards the sound of an Irish jig. Reaching the stage Jack saw that there were four strange creatures with the head and arms of an old man, but the body and rear of something like a horse or a goat. One held a harp and pulled gently at its strings, producing a delicate soothing harmony; a second played a fiddle, by turns gracefully leading the notes on their dance, and then running full tilt with discordant warlike screeches. The two other Phooka were performing a curious mixture of dances: initially courteous, a formal sequence of steps and bows, with elegant sweeps of the arm, then upright, fierce-eyed and haughty, stamping their hooves and daring the other to advance further.

Jack had never seen Phooka before, and their half-serious half-comic routine fascinated him. The routine rose to a climax, with the two Phooka advancing slowly on each other, their arms raised in defiance and threat.

One made as if to strike the other . . .

Aaargh!

Startled out of his reverie, Jack could hear screaming from the north side of Falabray. The Hobshee had arrived.

7
Kedge and Ploutter

The morning after the festival, Petros led the youngsters out to the High Street, and they spent a happy two or three hours trying to identify the languages and strange clothes of the various tourist groups.

"What about that lot?" said Petros. "German?"

"I've heard German before, and that isn't it," said Rana confidently. "They're Swedish."

"There were some trolls over from Sweden once," announced Lizzie. "Dad told me. They were small and hairy, and they smelt terrible."

"That wasn't Sweden, that was Norway," chimed in Rana.

"Close enough," replied her sister crossly.

"Close enough for you, dimwit," said Rana, and received a hard shove back.

"Hiya, Petros, Jack."

The four youngsters turned to see who had spoken. Across the street were two Shian youths, sitting with their backs against a shop wall.

"It's Kedge and Ploutter," said Petros. "They must be up in town for a bit of fun. We'd better go and say hello."

"I've never liked Kedge," said Rana as they began to cross the road. "Not since he tried to hex me for borrowing his cards."

"Yes, well, your version of borrowing is what others call stealing," explained Petros patiently.

Kedge and Ploutter, raised on a Shian farm near Rangie, had not gone through a formal apprenticeship, instead learning farming from their large extended family. Strong, healthy lads, they had the appetite for merriment and high jinks of the nearly adult.

"D'ye fancy a bit o' fun?" Kedge stood up.

"Too right," said Petros. "What are we doing?"

"We should be getting home," said Lizzie firmly. "We've people coming for lunch."

"Ye've time for an echo hex, though, haven't ye?" said Ploutter.

"What kind of hex?" asked Jack.

"Echo hex. Ye bounce it aff a wall," replied Kedge. "Come on, we'll go up the street a bittie. It works best the closer we are to the Stone."

"Aye," confirmed Kedge. "Even a couple of years ago this wouldn't have worked well. But the Stone's gettin' stronger all the time."

They all walked up the street to where it narrowed.

"This is a good spot," said Kedge. "Plenty o' gaps between the cars. What'll we start with?"

"How about a spinner?" said Ploutter.

"A what?" asked Rana.

"Spinner. Look, we'll show ye."

The two lads stood with their backs to the wall on one side of the road and waited for a group of tourists to approach. As they did, Ploutter held up his right palm and fired a hex across the street. It hit the far wall at an angle, and bounced back across the street, encountering nothing in its path.

"Ya eejit." Kedge shoved Ploutter aside, then raised his own right hand, palm facing across the road. The hex hit the far wall, careering into a group of four young tourists. Two of them appeared to slip, spinning round frantically before crashing down onto the pavement. Their friends looked on and started to laugh at this pratfall.

"See? Even the humans think it's funny," said Kedge. Jack began to laugh.

"I want to try my firestone now," said Ploutter. "I bought it aff a flame spirit at the Seventh."

Ploutter waited until three cars approached. Springing forward, he threw a small red stone in front of the first car, which was enveloped in a sheet of flame. Instinctively, the driver of the second car slammed his brakes on, and was rear-ended by the third car. As the front and rear lights of the two cars shattered, the flames on the first car disappeared. The driver of the third car got out and hammered on the window of the car in front, demanding an explanation. Ploutter and Kedge roared with laughter.

"That's not funny!" shouted Lizzie. "They haven't done *you* any harm."

Jack watched as the second car driver huddled nervously in his car, and various onlookers gathered to offer their advice. He had to admit that the spinning hex had been much funnier.

"We'd better get out o' here," said Kedge. "See you guys later."

He and Ploutter ran off down the road away from the castle, leaving Jack and the others watching the scene in front of them with bewilderment. Only Petros seemed untroubled, but he knew better than to get caught for someone else's pranks.

"Let's get up to the esplanade," he said. "It's best not to stick around."

"That wasn't exactly clever," said Lizzie. "Making someone spin was funny, even the humans were laughing at that. But making those cars crash, that's just stupid."

"Kedge and Ploutter *are* stupid," agreed Rana. "And so much for not drawing attention to yourself. They're bound to get caught."

"It must be nice to know those hexes, though, 'specially as they work better with the Stone nearby," mused Petros. "Could be useful one day."

Jack changed the subject. "Can we try some ice cream? I'll pay."

Leading them towards a kiosk, he put his hand into his pocket. Petros moved in front of him and shook his head.

"How're you going to pay?" he asked quietly. "They don't take silver shillings here. Human money's different. Didn't Dad say?"

Jack dreaded to think how Rana and Lizzie would have teased him if they'd found out. Fortunately, they were too busy arguing about trolls to have noticed.

"Watch," said Petros. "It's not difficult."

Petros joined the front of a queue waiting at the kiosk, and Jack saw him take in a couple of deep breaths and cough loudly. To Jack's amazement, Petros seemed to become a little bigger, more *there*. The woman standing behind him blinked, and anxiously stepped back a little to create room, as he placed some coins on the counter.

Petros handed round the ice creams and they made their way towards the esplanade. Jack took a couple of licks, and spat in disgust.

"Don't you like it?" said Petros. "Most Shian can't eat human food. I'll eat yours. We're all right because Mum's dad was human. Speaking of Mum, she'll be wondering where we are. D'you know who's coming for lunch?"

"We must be going," said their neighbour Festus as the meal drew to a close. "I said I'd show the girls the castle from the outside."

As he laughed at his little joke, his daughters Freya and Purdy expressed their feelings with a look of experienced resignation.

Jack showed them out and traipsed slowly back into the kitchen. Throughout the meal, he had avoided eye contact with his uncle and grandfather, fearful of recriminations after the previous night's outburst. With the visitors now away, he was predicting a dressing-down. As he entered the kitchen, his grandfather stood up. Jack looked fearfully at him, then at his uncle, but there was no hint of anger on either's face.

"Last night didn't end quite the way I'd hoped, young Jack. But I hope now that you understand a bit more about why your mother left."

"I think so. But whenever I asked anyone before, they just changed the subject."

"Sometimes youngsters grow up faster than we realise, young Jack."

"Grandpa," began Jack. "Could ... could you just call me 'Jack'? I'm not a kid any more."

"Of course. 'Jack' it is. And as a mark of how much we think you can handle yourself, why don't you and the others go up to Keldy to see Ossian? You've a few days before you start your apprenticeship. Uncle Hart will make sure you're safe."

"How are we going to get up there?"

"It's taken some time, but the Stone's opening up a lot of the low roads again."

"Can't we stay here?" complained Petros. "There's nothing to do in Keldy."

Although Ossian and his family had visited Rangie many times, Jack had never been to Keldy before. He had heard many stories about the loch, and the strange Shian that lived in the woods. His eyes glowed with excitement.

I'm going on the low road!

8
Keldy

Two days later, Uncle Doonya led the youngsters down behind an unoccupied cottage at the bottom of the square. In the corner of the gloomy garden was a mound of earth. Doonya corralled the four youngsters until they were all standing on it in a circle, facing inwards. Jack's heart began to race.

"Come along! Put your arms through your bag straps, and hold hands," said Doonya firmly, raising his arms so that his cloak covered the others. "Otherwise you could end up anywhere."

"Just a minute!" called Rana. "We've left Nuxie behind."

She scampered quickly back to the house and returned two minutes later cradling the small creature.

"Wind-flock Keldy," intoned Uncle Doonya.

A loud low whisper reverberated, and Jack began to feel his whole body spinning. His head whirled faster and faster, and instinctively he closed his eyes to stop himself feeling sick. The low whisper increased to a drone, with moaning and wailing mixed in. An eerie sound, it reminded Jack of times when someone had died at Rangie and the local Shian gathered to mourn. He felt dizzy. When he opened his mouth, he found he couldn't speak.

The drone had become a whine, and suddenly Jack felt as if he was flying. The gloom of the garden had gone. Cautiously he opened his eyes, and through the flapping of his uncle's cloak, was aware of light slipping past at great speed.

It seemed like hours before things slowed down, but gradually the whine dropped in pitch. With a jolt he recognised Lizzie's voice.

"Are we nearly there? I feel sick."

What had been blurs came into proper focus, and the spinning and whining slowed right down.

"Everyone all right? We've arrived." Uncle Doonya lowered his cloak.

Jack looked around him and saw that Lizzie still had her eyes firmly closed.

"Come on, Lizzie." Petros was grinning. "We're here."

Lizzie warily opened her eyes, but her pale face revealed her continuing nausea.

"That was horrible," she gasped. "I want to lie down."

"You'll be fine," said her father. "It's a strange feeling, but it'll soon pass. We've travelled seventy miles in under ten minutes. How are you, Rana? And you, Jack?"

"I feel all right," said Rana. "That was weird, though, wasn't it? Like being a spinning top."

Jack didn't feel quite as brave as Rana sounded, but wasn't about to admit this.

"Come on," said Petros, "the house isn't far." He pointed to a track that led away from the gate. "There's Ossian now. Hey! We're here!" He waved at a distant figure, which began running towards them.

Jack hadn't seen his older cousin Ossian since a visit to Rangie several months earlier. Ossian came running along, an agile, healthy-looking lad of fifteen.

"How're you doin'?" he called, while still ten or twenty yards away. "Enjoy the trip?"

"Lizzie feels sick," said Rana heartlessly. "I thought it was fun. D'you like going on the low road?"

"I do it all the time," he answered casually. "You meet up with all sorts. How're you doin', Rabbit?"

Jack groaned inwardly at Ossian's joke. A couple of years earlier, Ossian had heard Aunt Katie repeatedly saying 'Jack dear'; since then, he'd decided that 'Jack Rabbit' was a better name than 'Jack *deer*'. Jack looked up to his big cousin, but the joke had worn off.

"Hurry up! We'll get up to the house," said Doonya. "Lizzie may have to rest for a while."

Jack gloried in the scent of the cornfields, the feeling of truly fresh air on his face. The buzzing of insects was a soothing contrast to the harsh city sounds he'd lately grown used to.

"Come away in, you lot." Aunt Dorcas stood by the door. "Petros, show Jack where the bedrooms are. Just dump your bags; lunch is ready."

Aunt Dorcas, thought Jack happily, *does not stand on ceremony*. And her cooking, based on what she had brought on various trips to Rangie, was a whole lot better than Aunt Katie's.

Jack's eyes opened wide as he wandered through the large house.

"There's just the three of you here?" he asked incredulously. The dining room alone looked as big as the whole ground floor of the houses in Edinburgh.

"I hate bein' cramped," replied Ossian. "I couldn't live under that castle, I need room."

"But Edinburgh's great, Ossian," said Petros. "There's wicked things to do there. There's the people, and all the shops. The humans have some cool stuff."

Lunch was eaten amid happy chatter. Jack cleared his plate quickly. Aunt Dorcas's cooking was *superb* – even Lizzie was eating heartily.

The meal over, Dorcas shooed the youngsters away. "Ossian, show your cousins around. But Jack's not to go too far, and don't any of you touch any of the toadstools and mushrooms."

"Yes, Auntie," chorused Rana and Lizzie.

"Mum already warned us about them," added Petros.

"I'll show you the loch first," said Ossian, leading the others outside.

"Can we go fishing?" asked Rana, trying to keep up with her big cousin.

"Sure," replied Ossian. "I've got some rods."

Squatting down by a large tree, Ossian reached inside the trunk's hollow base and withdrew two fishing rods.

"I got these ready earlier. Come on, the loch's just around this corner."

As they turned the bend in the track, the great expanse of Loch Keldy spread out before them. Jack's eyes sparkled with excitement.

"Now, if you girls set up here by the bridge, there's somethin' I want to show the boys."

Ossian led Jack and Petros down below the bridge, where a small boat was tied up. They clambered in, and Ossian started rowing out onto the great loch.

9

The Kelpie and the Oakshee

After several minutes, Ossian stopped rowing.

"That's Lawse Mountain." He nodded towards a great hill that rose above the loch. "And over there's the Dameve village. We mostly keep away from them."

"'Dameve village'?" asked Jack.

Ossian looked at him closely. "It means 'human', but don't say it near Dad. Come on, I'll show you somethin'."

They were near the far side of the loch now. Ossian shipped the oars inside the boat, which bobbed up and down gently. Taking a small bottle out of his pocket, he dribbled the contents over the side. After a minute or so, he called out softly, "Hicka, hicka, yakooshk."

Jack and Petros watched in wonder as the water around the boat started to tremble. Suddenly, a horse's head broke the surface of the water.

"It's a kelpie!" yelped Petros.

"Shh!" urged Ossian. "He doesn't know you yet."

Ossian muttered soothing sounds – were they words? – that neither Jack nor Petros understood. The kelpie seemed reassured, for it remained with its face above the surface. Then, to Jack and Petros's astonishment, it appeared to be talking back.

Jack whispered to Petros, "I've never seen a kelpie before. Is it safe?"

"It's a water horse," answered Petros out of the corner of his mouth, clearly not wanting to upset the creature. "They're dangerous to Dameves, but they're usually fine with Shian."

You're a quarter Dameve yourself, if it comes to that, thought Jack, but said nothing. Ossian and the kelpie carried on their strange conversation.

"I've told him you're my cousins," Ossian said sternly. "He's heard about you, Jack."

Jack's eyes nearly popped out of his head. "How can he have heard of me?!"

"He's heard about your father. He says there are creatures nearby who know what happened."

Ossian avoided looking at Jack, who sensed this was not the whole story. Jack was caught in a dilemma. Did he want to know the truth, whatever it was? Quickly he made his mind up.

"Who? If there's anyone here who knows more, I want to meet them."

"It's no' that simple," replied Ossian evasively. "The creatures he talked about bide in the woods; some o' them don't like visitors."

"I still want to see them," stated Jack emphatically. "If they know what happened to my father then I'm entitled to know."

"Do we have to go?" asked Petros. "Maybe we should get Dad or Uncle Hart to come with us."

"We don't need any of the adults," Jack insisted. "You know your way around the woods, don't you, Ossian?"

Ossian's pride was at stake. "All right. But you have to do what I say. No' everyone in there welcomes visitors."

He began rowing over to the other side of the loch. Reaching the water's edge, the boys clambered out, and Ossian silently led the way up into the woods. Jack couldn't resist shuffling the dead leaves on the ground, but Ossian turned round and glared at him to stop. After fifteen minutes or so, he paused and held up his hand. Jack and Petros halted abruptly, neither making any sound. Turning round, Ossian motioned to them to remain still. He then edged slowly towards a large oak. Standing erect, he called out in what he hoped was an authoritative voice, "I am Ossian. I crave the wisdom o' the spirit o' this great tree."

After a minute or two, the leaves of the tree began to shake, and a soft rumbling came up from the ground.

"I am Ossian, son o' Hart. I wish to consult the spirit."

The rumbling faded. Then, from somewhere deep inside the trunk, a booming voice came. "Speak, Ossian, son o' Hart. But tell me, who are these strangers ye've broucht?"

"Spirit, these are my cousins from Rangie. The great kelpie told me that you know what happened to Jack's father, Phineas o' Rangie."

"The kelpie had nae business tae be tellin' ye this, Ossian, son o' Hart. And ye're very bold tae come this way yersel'."

"But can you tell him anythin'?" Ossian persisted.

There was silence. Then, out of the corner of his eye, Jack noticed a tree root emerge slowly from the ground and edge towards Ossian's feet. He stared in disbelief then suddenly darted forward, pulling his cousin back.

"Look out, Ossian!"

Ossian saw the root and instinctively leapt back, but instead of retreating with him, Jack stood there defiantly. Petros took half a pace forward, his arm out to restrain Jack, then stepped back.

"I am Jack Shian from Rangie," Jack called. "We have come for information. If you can tell me where my father is, I shall be grateful."

For a moment there was silence. Jack's initial courage began to waver. Then the spirit spoke again.

"Ye're also bold, Jack Shian. Would ye tak' the punishment that should have gone tae yer cousin?"

"I would," replied Jack, his boldness returning. "But I seek information. Do you have the information I ask for?"

Another pause.

"Yer bravery does ye credit," the tree spirit said at last. "But the water horse exaggerated. Aye, the Oakshee hear mony things, and Phineas from Rangie *was* travelling north wi' Konan the Brashat some years ago. They made camp near here, but mair than that I canna say. There are ithers who may ken mair than I. Seek ye Tamlina."

After a pause, the voice came again. "Now go. Jack o' Rangie, yer courage will tak' ye far. As for ye, Ossian, son o' Hart, tak' care. There are ways o' consultin' the Oakshee. This time, ye may leave in peace."

As the tree root disappeared, Jack turned to face the others.

"Let's get out of here."

Petros watched Jack sullenly as they walked along. While he admired his bravery, he resented Jack's having taken the limelight. Unsure of what to say to Jack, Petros turned on Ossian instead as they untied the boat.

"What did you do to upset it, Ossian? I thought you knew your way around these woods."

"I do. But we should've sent someone ahead to let the Oakshee know we were comin'. Like I said, they don't always like visitors." As he rowed, Ossian kept his eyes fixed firmly on his own feet.

Who was Tamlina? Jack had heard the name before, but where? His grandfather? *And how could she know about his father?* It grated that others knew more than he did.

As the boat approached the bridge, Ossian looked up at Jack. He gulped once or twice before muttering, "Thanks."

"No more 'Rabbit', then. OK?"

Ossian nodded.

10
Tamlina

The next few days passed in a haze of sunshine, rowing on the loch and playing on the outskirts of the woods. But all too soon the final day came, and after lunch Jack and the others went upstairs to pack. As Jack and Petros came downstairs, Ossian appeared at the front door.

"I've a surprise for you. Come on, it'll take a while to get there."

Rana and Lizzie bounded down the stairs, each trying to reach the bottom first.

"Where are *you* going?" called out Rana.

"Shhh!" hissed Ossian, glancing nervously towards the kitchen. His face registered dismay as his mother appeared.

"Where are you off to? Mind that they're leaving before suppertime."

"I'm just goin' to show them the waterfall again," said Ossian. "We'll be back soon."

"Well, don't be long. Jack and Petros start work tomorrow, they mustn't be late."

The boys made their way outside, but were inevitably followed by Rana and Lizzie.

"Where are we going?" asked Lizzie.

"What d'you mean, 'we'?" said Ossian. "This is boys' stuff. You can go and play by yourselves."

"If you don't let us come along, we'll tell Aunt Dorcas," said Rana simply.

Seeing that he had been out-manoeuvred, Ossian motioned to the girls to follow. Although his pace was fast for them, they knew that complaining was not an option. A good fifteen minutes later Ossian stopped and turned round.

"We're goin' to see someone," he stated simply. "And you've to swear not to tell Dad. He'll go spare if he finds out, so you'll all be in trouble too. Got that?" The others indicated assent.

"Jack," continued Ossian, "d'you remember the Oakshee mentionin' Tamlina? Well, I've found out where she is today."

"What were the Oakshee like?" asked Rana, wide-eyed. "Dad says they can be dangerous."

"Never heed them now," said Ossian irritably. "I've sent a grig ahead to let her know we're comin'. We don't want a repeat o' last time."

"Who *is* Tamlina?" asked Jack. "I'm sure I've heard the name before somewhere."

"She's the Enchantress," explained Ossian. "And today she's comin' to collect plants near here. A Ghillie-Doo told me last night."

"A what?" said Petros.

"Ghillie-Doo. They're tree guardians, they hear all sorts o' things. One o' them told me last night that Tamlina's goin' to be near here today."

"D'you talk to trees a lot, then?" laughed Rana.

Ossian's eyes narrowed.

"Just because you've no' met different Shian in your cosseted wee life doesn't mean they're no' important. This one knows a lot more than you, for a start."

Rana blushed, and averted her gaze.

"Which plants is she collecting?" asked Lizzie, breaking the awkward silence.

"There's hawthorn here, but she does all sorts – could be almost anythin'."

Reaching a small clearing, Ossian stopped. "We'll wait here. The grig'll find us."

"A grig's like a pixie, right?" said Lizzie. "Mum told me. They're friendly."

"It's not 'pixie', it's 'pisgie'," snorted Rana. "Only humans call them pixies."

Ossian withdrew a small pot of heather honey from his pocket. "We'll have to pay her; they like this."

They all sat down in the clearing and waited. Small insects buzzed in the sunlight, and Jack started to feel sweat trickle down the back of his neck. He swiped irritably at the midges.

"Have you met Tamlina?" he asked Ossian. "What's she like?"

"I've seen her once. She doesn't go out o' her way to meet people, but if we're lucky she'll maybe tell us somethin'."

After what seemed like an eternity, Jack heard a faint whirring sound. There weren't any grigs in Rangie, and he wasn't quite sure what to expect.

A tiny winged creature flew towards them, no bigger than Jack's hand. It flew straight to Ossian, and hovered in front of him, performing a bee-like dance. Ossian nodded.

"She's nearby. She knew we were comin', but at least she doesn't think we're tryin' to sneak up on her. Nobody's to speak unless she asks a direct question, and be careful about lookin' her in the eye."

They made their way cautiously across the clearing and carried on along a barely discernible path. Little sunlight filtered down this far. They had walked only a couple of minutes when a young sapling fell across their path.

"That's far enough!" commanded a voice.

Jack looked, but couldn't see who was speaking. His heart started to beat more quickly, and the sweat now ran down his back.

"Yer grig telt me ye were comin', Ossian, son o' Hart. Ye dinna usually venture intae the woods this far. Whit brings ye here?"

Ossian looked vainly to see where the voice was coming from. As had happened when the Oakshee had tried to grab his ankles, Ossian didn't – or couldn't – speak. On impulse, Jack stepped forward, his blue eye flashing in the gloomy light.

"I am Jack Shian from Rangie," he announced. "The Oakshee told us you might know what has happened to my father, Phineas of Rangie."

He paused, unsure if he was facing in quite the right direction. Gradually, an old woman appeared in front of him. She wore a black full-length cloak, but her head was uncovered. Her eyes were set deep in her worn, creased face, and her hair was matted and dirty, its true colour unknowable. Jack guessed that she was old, but he had no idea how old.

"Ye're a bold creature tae walk this far intae the woods," she said, staring at Jack.

Excitement and nervousness competed within Jack. *Was that a compliment or a warning?*

"Aye, I've heard o' yer father," continued Tamlina, in her powerful voice. "Tamlina sees all. Whit dae ye want o' me?"

"Is he alive? Where is he?" The questions exploded out. Unsure what to expect, Jack hadn't prepared a speech. "I just want to know where he is."

Tamlina stared intently, as if appraising Jack's worth. Then she nodded.

"Come along, and bring the lassies wi' ye. The ithers can bide here." Her voice was authoritative. She turned and started to walk away.

"Where ..." Jack began, but a ferocious look from the old woman halted him. Her eyes seemed to bore right through him. Unable to hold her gaze, he looked down. Tamlina snorted, turned and swept away. Jack glanced back, and drawing on his reserves of courage motioned to Rana and Lizzie to follow.

Tamlina stopped abruptly beneath an old oak, and turned round. A black pot bubbled away over a small fire, a sharp, acrid smell rising from it. Lizzie, glancing back nervously, saw that Petros and Ossian were just in sight.

Tamlina picked up a long wooden spoon and stirred the contents of the pot, muttering to herself. Jack, Rana and Lizzie shuffled awkwardly, unsure of what to do.

"Sit doon, sit doon," barked Tamlina, apparently aware of their unease. "I'm jist makkin' some broth. Mebbe ye'd like tae try some?"

Rana and Lizzie exchanged anxious glances. Their unease increased as Tamlina dropped three large mushrooms into the pot. The broth sizzled briefly, and steam rose up, partially obscuring Tamlina's face.

"We'd love to," announced Jack, glaring pointedly at his cousins. Rana and Lizzie looked nervous, but said nothing. Tamlina clicked her fingers, and four leather goblets appeared in front of her. Pouring a small measure of broth into each, she handed them round. Jack blew gently into his goblet and waited.

"Ye're wantin' to find oot whit becam' o' young Phineas o' Rangie?"

Jack felt the hairs on the back of his neck bristle. He glanced at his cousins, who sat transfixed; neither had touched the broth given to them. Tamlina, gazing above their heads, seemed unaware of their presence. Abstractedly, she took a deep draught of the broth, slurping the fluid around in her mouth. Slowly, a look of intense concentration came upon her face, as if she gazed far back through the years. She began to speak, but her voice was quite different. The firm, commanding into-nation had gone, replaced by a low mumble – it was almost as if she was a different woman. Jack, Rana and Lizzie all sat forward to try and catch her words.

"Tamlina has seen many sorrows. Only the Grey has seen more than she. Foolish Shian and devils from Adam's race all seek the Stone . . . Thoughtless of the Trinity, all pursue its power . . . Young Phineas of Rangie and Konan the Brashat, trying to trick each other as they

passed through Keldy . . . Neither saw the danger . . . If sphere and silver they would gain, the Seat of Power they would attain . . ."

Her voice trailed off, her gaze still vacant.

Jack nudged Rana, and showed her that he was tipping out the contents of his goblet. Catching on, Rana followed suit, and indicated to Lizzie to do the same. Jack saw with some alarm that the dried leaves onto which the broth had been poured sizzled briefly. Hurriedly each picked up some loose earth and covered the evidence.

They needn't have hurried; it was fully two minutes before Tamlina emerged from her trance. She blinked slowly and cleared her throat, looking curiously at the three in front of her. For a moment she appeared not to recognise them. As realisation dawned, her manner and voice returned to what for her passed as normal.

"Tamlina sees that ye all ha'e learnt much this day. Did I speak o' the Raglan Stone?"

The youngsters all shook their heads.

"Be shrewd with yer wisdom, young anes, for wi' knowledge comes responsibility." Her voice was strong and confident.

"You said they were trying to trick each other," said Rana. "But what happened?"

"Foolish girl!" boomed the old woman, standing up quickly. "Dinna presume tae question Tamlina, she wha's seen a thoosan' tales unfold. Now, begone!"

And in a flash, she disappeared, together with all traces of the pot and the fire.

Rana looked stunned. Jack quickly got to his feet and grabbed her arm and Lizzie's. "Let's get back to the others."

As they walked hurriedly back the short distance to Petros and Ossian, Lizzie said, "D'you think she remembers what she said? It was like she was in a trance."

"What were those mushrooms she put in the broth?" Rana pulled a *yeuch* face. "I'm glad we didn't drink any of that."

"It must've been a potion," said Jack. "She *was* in a trance. When she came to, she didn't even know who we were."

"Did you see the ring on her finger?" asked Lizzie. "It was round with a strange pattern."

"I saw that," said Rana. "I couldn't make out what the pattern was. Did you see it, Jack?"

"Why couldn't I come with you?" asked Petros moodily as they approached.

"Were *you* going to argue with her?" demanded Jack. The nervousness he had felt earlier on had given way to relief now that they were away from the Enchantress.

As they walked back through the woods, Jack, Rana and Lizzie recounted the story of the broth, and what Tamlina had said.

"You didn't drink any o' it, did you?" said Ossian. "There's strange things growin' in here. I reckon she uses some o' them to get into a trance. But she's hundreds o' years old, she can deal with stuff like that; it might kill you."

"Is she really that old?" enquired Lizzie.

"She's been around for centuries," said Ossian. "She knows everythin' that happens around here. I don't know what she meant by Uncle Phineas and the Brashat tryin' to trick each other, though. And 'sphere and silver', and 'the Seat of Power', I've no idea what that is."

"The Icelandic elves told a story about a globe the other night," said Jack. "Could that be the sphere?"

"Who knows?" said Petros. "It could be a football for all we know. And what's the Seat of Power?"

"That used to mean a king's throne," stated Rana, "or the most powerful people in the land. How would you gain that?"

They had reached the edge of the woods. As they neared Ossian's house they saw his mother standing by the front door.

"And where have you been?" she demanded.

"The waterfall ..." began Ossian, but his mother held up her hand.

"You needn't try any of those tales with me, Ossian. Domovoy's been down that way all afternoon, and he hasn't seen hide nor hair of any of you."

"I asked if we could go and find some Oakshee," said Jack. "We don't have them in Rangie. I wanted to know what they're like."

Aunt Dorcas looked hard at Jack, trying to judge whether this bore any resemblance to the truth. Sensing that further enquiries would be unproductive, she said, "Come away in. You'll need to get your things together."

As Ossian made to follow the others, his mother put her arm across the doorway, blocking his route. Ossian was taller than his mother now, and much stronger. She looked at him, her eyes seeking some point of contact. Ossian stared back. Aware that this particular battle was lost, she lowered her arm, and watched sadly as her son passed into the house.

Once they had collected their belongings, Ossian led the others outside. They strode purposefully towards the wooden gate that led to the low road entrance. Doonya and Hart, in earnest discussion, emerged more slowly.

Looking over his shoulder, Ossian said, "It's all right, Dad. I'll take them back. I know the way."

"Dad!" called Rana. "Can you bring Nuxie? I left him in the bedroom."

Doonya waved a hand to show that he had heard.

As the youngsters reached the gate, Ossian stopped and turned round.

"D'you fancy goin' to a party?" he said. "You've hours yet, it's no' even suppertime."

Jack looked quizzically at him. "What kind of party?"

"The fun kind," replied Ossian testily. "Who's up for it?"

"I am," said Petros. "Work's a doddle, I can handle it. Where are we going?"

"It's all right," said Ossian, seeing Rana and Lizzie look doubtful. "It's no' far from the castle. You can go back whenever you want."

"OK ..." said Rana slowly. "But Mum's expecting us, and Dad's just behind, so he'll know if we've gone somewhere else."

The five stepped up to the mound, and Ossian put his cloak around the others.

"Wind-flock Cos-Howe," he said.

A loud low whisper reverberated, and Jack felt himself starting to spin.

11
Cos-Howe

The spinning stopped, and Jack's nausea quickly settled. Ossian's cloak was still around the others, but Jack could see that they were in a dark chamber, lit only by two burning torches.

"Told you I'd get you here all right," announced Ossian with evident satisfaction. "Let's get inside."

"Wait a minute," said Rana. "Lizzie's feeling sick again."

"Come on," said Petros encouragingly. "We'll find you somewhere to sit down."

He led Lizzie as they all made their way towards a great wooden door at the end of the gloomy chamber. It was very different from the Shian square, with its shafts of light coming down from the crystals.

"Where exactly are we?" Jack asked.

"Cos-Howe," said Ossian. "For years this was only really a cave where local Shian met sometimes. But the Stone's opened it up again, so they're havin' a party. I didn't tell you before because I didn't want you tellin' my parents."

"Why?" challenged Rana. "What's wrong with them knowing we've gone to a party?"

"Let's just say they don't exactly approve o' some o' my friends," replied Ossian cagily. "Anyway, we're no' that far from the castle if you really want to go back."

"We're in Edinburgh again?" asked Rana. "It took longer to get up to Keldy."

"You're just gettin' used to it," answered Ossian. "Come on, the party's started."

The noise coming through the great wooden door confirmed that a party was indeed underway. A young man of about seventeen appeared.

"So, you've turned up, have you?"

"These are my cousins from Rangie. This is Petros and Jack, and Petros's sisters. Lizzie doesn't feel well."

The young man opened the door fully and motioned them in. "I hope you brought something."

On cue, Ossian produced a bottle from within his cloak.

"My mother's. It's good stuff."

Rana looked suspiciously at Ossian. "Did you steal that from home?"

"Mum makes it to be drunk, so what's the problem?"

"What is it?" asked Jack.

"Heather wine," replied Ossian. "It's quite bitter, but you get used to it. Let's find a table."

He led the way into the main room, a full twenty yards long, where the party was in full swing. Burning torches on the wall provided the only illumination. Tables had been pushed along each side, with others scattered around the centre. Single chairs, some upright, others on their side, were strewn haphazardly about. Groups of young men and women were talking, singing or playing games of chance. A strange musical blend of melodies and refrains could be heard from flutes, fiddles, guitars, and mandolins; none seemed to be playing the same tune.

"I'll go and say hi to a few people," explained Ossian, finding a spare table. "Wait here. I wouldn't talk to too many folk just yet. They've got to find out who you are."

Jack reckoned that the forty or fifty young men and women were between about fifteen and twenty, the men outnumbering the women. The flickering light of the torches gave a slightly eerie glow to the place. The noise was loud, but not overwhelming.

My first proper party, thought Jack. *Cool.*

From the end of the room came the smell of roasted food. Jack's stomach rumbled. Lunch seemed a long time ago.

"Where did Ossian say this place was?" asked Rana.

"Cos-Howe," replied her brother. "I think it's only a couple of miles from the castle, but I don't know the way."

"So we're stuck here?" asked Lizzie, feeling a little better.

Ossian reappeared, carrying a tray of drinks and food.

"I've told people you're here, and it's no problem," he announced, setting the tray down on the table. "There you go, some juniper juice for you." Turning to a young man at the next table, he continued, "Hi, Toozy. Any chance o' gettin' in on the cards?"

Jack didn't recognise the card game being played by the group of four young men next to them.

"Sure, pull up a chair."

Gratefully, Ossian pushed his chair along to the next table.

"Are you just going to leave us, then?" demanded Rana.

"It's OK, you can mingle now. I told you, people know who you are."

"But *we* don't know who *they* are," said Rana indignantly. "And they're all much older than us."

"Come on," said Petros to Jack. "We'll see if we can join another card game. You get the tray. You two had better come with us," he added to his sisters.

Rana and Lizzie got up from their chairs with no hint of enthusiasm, and followed the boys as they wandered along the line of tables. Seeing one group of card players that did not appear too raucous, Petros approached.

"We're Ossian's cousins. Can we join you?"

The young man was about seventeen, with hair down past his shoulders. He peered into Petros's face for a few moments.

"You're a bit young for this place, aren't you?" It wasn't said aggressively, more matter-of-fact.

"I'm thirteen," replied Petros defensively. "I've been working for a year now."

The young man continued staring at him, then slowly looked round at Jack, Rana and Lizzie. The others at the table were watching with interest. Casually, the young man indicated with a sweep of his arm that they could sit down.

"I'm Oobit," he said simply. "This is Gandie, Tom and Radge."

Jack and Petros grabbed two chairs each and pulled them up to the table. Cautiously, Rana and Lizzie also sat down.

"D'you want in?" queried Oobit.

"What game is it?" asked Jack uncertainly.

"Hunt the Queen," replied Gandie, rubbing his hands together. "I hope you've brought your silver shillings, because I'm on hot form today."

Petros surreptitiously slipped a few coins into Jack's pocket, and they were dealt in on the following hand. Jack played cautiously, trying to copy what the others did, but he quickly lost his money. Petros was faring better, and over the next hour he accumulated a small mound of coins.

Suddenly Tom stood and slammed his cards down.

"Cheat!" He punched Radge on the side of the head.

Radge spun off his chair, clutching his ear and howling.

"Grab the money!" hissed Rana to Petros, who appeared stunned. Jack stepped forward, scooped up Petros's winnings and retreated.

Tom and Radge began flailing at each other, uttering threats and curses in equal measure. To Jack's surprise, Oobit and Gandie just looked on and made no attempt to intervene.

"Shouldn't we stop them?" he asked.

"Why?" replied Oobit. "Radge is always cheating. It's time he was taught a lesson."

A tall fair-haired muscular man came over. He watched as Radge and Tom tried unsuccessfully to pin the other's arms to his side.

"Time for real wrestling, I think." The man had an air of authority, and Jack saw that Oobit simply nodded his agreement.

"Who's that?" Jack asked Gandie.

"Oh, that's Cosmo. He keeps things going here. Smart too – knows loads of stuff about stuff."

The man called Cosmo bent down, and with his powerful arms picked up the scuffling Radge and Tom. Both stopped struggling, but continued to glower at each other. Cosmo sat them both down and turned to face the centre of the large room. He swept his left arm slowly in front of him, and the upturned chairs and tables slid away to the side of the room. With a flick of his left hand, Cosmo pointed to the side walls. The number of blazing torches doubled.

This place is amazing, thought Jack.

The music and chatter died away quickly. Cosmo gestured to two young men of about sixteen, and each moved to the centre of the room. Rana and Lizzie had to squirm forward so that they could see. Jack remained at the back of the crowd and stood on a chair.

"What's happening?" said Petros to Oobit.

"Wrestling. We usually have a few contests before we go off to France."

12
Mascot Jack

The contest was quickly a one-sided affair. Flung onto his back once more, the smaller of the two young men snarled angrily. His opponent Davie, confident of victory, took time to look around and acknowledge his friends' cheers. Reaching into his shirt, the smaller man withdrew two shiny stones, and uttering a sharp cry he threw them to the floor. There was a flash of purple smoke, and his opponent sank to his knees, howling with pain.

In an instant Cosmo had stepped forward, holding out his left palm.

"*Eeshogel!*"

It was as if the smaller man had been frozen. He stood motionless, a startled look on his face. Several young men ran forward and helped Davie to the side of the room. He was holding his face and shouting that he couldn't see.

"What's happening?" asked Rana.

"You're not allowed to use hex stones," explained Oobit. "Rob could have blinded Davie."

The atmosphere had changed abruptly. From a raucous crowd shouting encouragement, it was now subdued. Rob, transfixed, could only move his eyes. From the chair on which he stood, Jack read Rob's face: terror.

Cosmo faced Rob, his expression one of complete contempt. Grabbing Rob's collar, he dragged him backwards, and threw him disdainfully into a corner.

"There will be no use of hexes in our contests," he announced emphatically. "I am sorry that our young guests have witnessed this breach of our rules. But let us continue. We cannot let this spoil our preparations."

Two more young men dutifully moved forward to the centre of the room and began to wrestle.

Over the next half hour Jack witnessed three further contests, all more evenly matched than the first. Cheers and applause greeted the end of each challenge, with the winner returning triumphantly to his friends and the loser retreating quietly to a side table where he could nurse his injuries and drown his sorrows.

The girls had a ringside view, but while Rana was spellbound by the action, Lizzie found it disturbing – and yet unmissable. Jack, enthralled by the contests, shouted encouragement along with everyone else. Noting his enthusiasm, Cosmo stepped forward after one particularly energetic bout, and held up his hand.

"My friends," he began. "These contests build us for our match tonight in France. I think we have time for one more bout. Ossian, come forward. And young Jack of Rangie, you shall challenge him."

Jack's heart almost stopped. He had been enjoying the contests, but had never considered taking part. Although Ossian was younger by a year or two than most of the Cos-Howe lads, he was bigger than several of them, and obviously much stronger than Jack.

"Come on, Jack," encouraged Cosmo. "You're not scared to wrestle your cousin, are you?"

Jack didn't notice as Cosmo winked slyly at Ossian. Climbing hesitantly down from his chair, Jack made his way to the centre of the room where Ossian stood, smiling. Slowly they circled each other, then Ossian darted forward and grabbed Jack's arms. Jack tried to wriggle, but soon found himself sprawling on the floor. While Ossian bowed grandly to the audience's ironic cheers, Jack quickly got to his feet and ran forward, gripping Ossian's waist. Taken by surprise, Ossian was briefly winded, and he staggered back, tripping and falling. Mocking cheers echoed around the room. Determined not to be humiliated by his smaller cousin, Ossian stood up and moving swiftly forward, twisted and threw Jack onto the floor.

Over the next five minutes, he systematically repeated this. Time after time, Jack fell with a back-crunching thump, and yet, even as his back begged him to lie there and concede, each time he got up and faced his big cousin. After what seemed the tenth time, he staggered to his feet again, but was having trouble focussing. Cosmo stepped forward and deftly parted them.

"A worthy contestant!" he shouted, to loud applause. "Determination like this is rare. We have a mascot for tonight!"

Ossian put his arm around Jack's shoulders. "Are you all right?" he asked anxiously. "You should've stayed down ages ago. If you get up, I've got to put you down again."

Jack tried to speak, but no sound came out. His legs were wobbling, and the pain across his back was excruciating. Rana ran forward and tried to hug him, which made him writhe in agony.

"How come you weren't picked?" She decided to take things out on her brother. "You're older, you should have taken Jack's place."

"He couldn't," explained Ossian. "Cosmo chose Jack, he'd no choice. And Jack made a good go o' it. I thought he'd stay down after the first couple o' throws. Look, I'll get him some heather wine, that'll pick him up."

Ossian returned a few moments later with two goblets full of wine.

"Your health, wee cousin!" He took a deep draught of the wine, and smacked his lips.

Jack took a sip, and immediately spluttered as the wine reached his throat.

"He shouldn't be having wine," shouted Lizzie indignantly. "Mum'll be furious if she finds out."

Petros gently released Jack's grip on the goblet and set it down. "You can have more later if you want some," he said. "Ossian, can I have a word?"

The pair stepped away from the table for a few moments. When they returned, Ossian pushed the goblet further away from Jack.

"Mebbe it's a bit strong. I just thought it would help you after the wrestlin'."

Jack's head was not ringing so much now. He looked at Rana and Lizzie, and smiled weakly.

"I'll be all right. Back's a bit sore, that's all."

Ossian sat and looked at Jack. "You sure you're all right? Cosmo was really impressed wi' the way you kept gettin' back up. He thinks you'll bring us luck tonight."

"What d'you mean?" asked Jack, slowly starting to get his thoughts in order. "Luck for what? And what was all that stuff about a mascot?"

"We're goin' to France for a game o' Shian football. We do it every year, to play for the King's Cup."

"But we're starting work tomorrow," said Jack. "We can't go anywhere else today."

"Tonight, you mean." Rana was getting annoyed. "We should've been at the castle ages ago."

"It's just a game o' football," said Ossian. "Cos-Howe against the Claville boys. They've been doin' it for years. 'Course, the Stone bein' back has made the journey a lot easier."

"We're already late," Lizzie sided with her sister. "What'll Mum think?"

"I'll send a grig to let her know we're OK," said Ossian. "The grig can take the bags as well."

"How will a grig carry all our bags?" asked Rana incredulously.

"Wi' a charm, o' course," replied Ossian testily. "Now, has anyone got anythin' to pay her?"

Petros reached into his pocket and took out a tiny coin. "Is that enough?" he asked.

"That's fine. I won't be long."

Ossian, however, was gone for ages. The party continued, and every now and then someone would come up and compliment Jack on his courage. Jack's back still ached, but the glow of the praise had a remarkably painkilling effect. He took another sip of the wine, and this time it did not burn his mouth.

Jack was basking in the unaccustomed feeling of being praised for his bravery, when one of the Cos-Howe group came up. Expecting another compliment, Jack looked up eagerly. His anticipation, however, was misplaced.

"Kids," snarled the youth, and turned on his heel.

Jack blinked in astonishment. *What was all that about?*

Lizzie began to fidget, asking repeatedly what time it was. Petros tried to sound as if he was in control.

"I think the castle's about two miles away, but we could easily get lost. It'll be getting dark soon. Why don't we just hang out with Ossian and go and watch the game?"

"How are we getting to France?" asked Rana. "That's a long way. I want to go home."

"Ossian said the Stone had made the journey easier," stated Petros. "That's got to be worth trying."

There followed a heated discussion about the rights and wrongs of travelling to France. Eventually, Petros said to his sisters, "All right, you two can try and get back on your own. But don't say I didn't warn you. You'll get lost, and then what will you do?"

"Come on, it'll be fun," said Jack encouragingly. "How often will we get the chance to do this again?"

Ossian returned and informed them that a grig had been despatched to tell Aunt Katie that they were all all right. The music had died down, and Jack could see that people were starting to drift towards the great wooden door.

"How are we getting there?" he asked.

"Horse and hattock!" replied Ossian.

13
The Night Flight to France

Emerging through the great wooden door, Jack saw that about thirty people had congregated in the entrance chamber. Ossian was busy explaining to Petros about the history of the game against Claville. Rana and Lizzie followed reluctantly.

Cosmo, organising people into small groups, caught sight of Ossian.

"Can you get the others to France all right? You're good with horses."

Ossian indicated that this was no problem. He ushered them together to face the side wall of the chamber, ensuring they were all holding hands. Holding up his own right hand against the rock wall, he whispered, "*Effracto.*"

A section of the rock wall opened away from them, like a hinged door.

"Come on, quickly!" snapped Ossian.

Stepping smartly through the doorway, they changed back to human sizes again.

"You don't get very long," explained Ossian. "That's why you do it in small groups. But we need to be human-size to get the horses."

"Where are we getting the horses from?" Rana's excitement at the prospect of riding was enough to make her forget her earlier concerns.

"Down here." Ossian set off at a smart pace.

After crossing a couple of streets, they found themselves in a part of the city that was not built up. Around them to the left and right appeared to be grassland, and ahead of them was a hill.

"That's Arthur's Seat!" exclaimed Petros as he looked up.

"The back o' it," corrected Ossian. "Come on, it's no' far."

"Can't we get home from here?" asked Lizzie. "I think I can remember the way."

Petros looked at the rising rock face in front of them. "No, we came down a different part of the slope. Anyway, you can't work the charm to get into the square yet."

Lizzie followed on, sulkily. Rana hung back a little, and left her alone. Skirting round the base of Arthur's Seat, they came to a low wall in deep shadow. Jack could just see that about twenty others were crouched down at the wall. Cosmo held his forefinger up to his lips. Dutifully, they fell silent, tiptoeing forward quietly.

"Three of us'll go in," stated Cosmo. "Ten horses should be enough."

"Ten horses for twenty-five of us?" whispered Rana.

"Shhh! Keep your voice down," hissed Ossian. "You'll see."

He followed Cosmo and one other as they vaulted the low wall.

"Where are the others?" said Jack. "There was more than this in the entrance hall."

"Dunno," Petros said blankly. "Maybe they're going another way."

"Are we just going to take the horses?" asked Lizzie.

"Are you still complaining?" retorted her brother.

"But taking them is stealing."

"Oh, unlike your 'finding' things up at the castle," said Petros. "Anyway, we're only borrowing them. Ossian said they'll be back before dawn."

"Dawn?" exclaimed Lizzie. "We're not staying up all night, are we?"

"'Course not. I just meant they'll be back in their stables before the humans know they've gone."

Jack was wondering what it would be like to stay up all night, when a low whistle from behind the wall made him start.

"Come on. You and me'll go together," whispered Petros. "Ossian'll take the girls."

"D'you mean I don't even get my own horse?" demanded Rana.

"Can *you* make it fly?" asked her brother sarcastically, as two horses came sailing silently over the wall.

"Up you get," said Ossian. He indicated to Rana to leave a space for Lizzie. Mounting quickly, Rana edged back on the saddle-less horse and helped her less confident sister up.

"Hold tight to my belt," said Ossian.

Jack and Petros both vaulted onto the back of the second horse. At a signal, all the horses proceeded forward at a trot along the base of Arthur's Seat. The trot quickly became a canter, then a gallop. As each mount reached full speed, its lead rider called out, "Horse and hattock!"

The sudden rise startled Jack. He gripped Petros's belt with all his might as the chilly wind whipped past him. Slowly, Jack got used to the sensation of speed and cold, and dared to open his eyes. Petros, holding tight to the horse's mane, looked around occasionally to check Jack was all right.

After thirty minutes, the horses began to descend. Looking down, Jack saw a trail of lights, a flame circle at its head. Within minutes, they had all landed in a small field ringed with Shian bearing torches. The horses were shuddering with the fear or thrill of the experience, but none made any sound. Each lead rider led his horse towards a small enclosure by the edge of the field. Left with some hay, the horses appeared none the worse for their flight.

"How did you like that?" asked Ossian, smiling.

Rana hugged him in reply. Lizzie, relieved to get down out of the cold wind, mumbled indistinctly. In fact, on ground level it was a pleasant summer's night.

"That was brilliant." Petros's eyes were gleaming. "What a rush, Jack!"

Jack *had* grown used to the flight, but still had a nagging feeling that he should have enjoyed it more.

"Welcome, *mes amis*!" A tall dark-haired man shook Cosmo's hand. "Are you in good form for tonight's game?"

"You're in for a surprise, Henri." Cosmo eyed him steadily. "We'll be taking the cup home with us tonight."

"Ah, ever the optimist," replied Henri happily. "Do you need time to get ready, or shall we start?"

Glancing round at the rest of the Cos-Howe group, Cosmo turned back to Henri. "Whenever you like."

14
Shian Football

Henri climbed onto the stone wall and signalled for silence.

"My friends, welcome to our game. Tonight we celebrate the five hundred and thirty-eighth match between Claville and Cos-Howe. I am pleased to see that our visitors have brought some young supporters along. For their benefit, our ancient town has two stone gateways, one north, one south. The team who scores first wins. Players may fly; charms and hexes must last no longer than two Shian minutes and must not cause lasting damage. Please disturb our human hosts as little as possible. We play for the honour of lifting the King's Cup."

Henri drew a sceptre from his cloak and sketched a thin line of flame in front of him, and whispered, "*Calixignis!*"

To Jack's astonishment the flickering flames created the outline of an ornate goblet. A great cheer greeted its appearance.

"Wow!" exclaimed Petros. "They must play for a fire cup each year."

"Yes, it is a copy," said a Claville player. "The real King's Cup disappeared years ago. They say one day the ghosts who made it will return, when the Cup is found."

"Grandpa didn't believe the King's Cup existed," stated Jack. "He said it was just a story about making the Stone's power stronger."

"It's not much use if it's only a fire copy," said Lizzie huffily.

"But it proves there is a real Cup – or at least was. You can't have a copy of something that never existed. That could be really powerful if we got it."

"Yeah, and really bad if the Brashat got it. Remember what they did at midsummer."

"Look at those markings," said Rana, indicating the decorations on the cup. "I've seen that pattern somewhere before."

"In accordance with our rules, the visitors may choose which gate they will defend," announced Henri.

"We'll take the north end," replied Cosmo. "Who'll look after our mascots?"

"My brother Philippe will take them. They will get a good view from the town hall tower." He motioned to a lad of about fifteen, who came forward.

"My cousin should go too," said a dark-haired youth from the Cos-Howe group. "He's not old enough to play."

Jack recognised the youth who had snarled at him back at Cos-Howe. Next to him stood a young lad about his own age. Cosmo strode up to the man who had spoken and hissed, "Who said you could bring your cousin, Grulsh?"

"Ossian's brought along some kids." Grulsh shrugged. "What's one more?"

Realising that a public argument was not in his team's best interests, Cosmo merely replied, "I'll see you after the game."

"I'm Fenrig."

The youngster stepped forward and stared at Jack and Petros. The statement had carried no hint of friendliness, and Jack experienced a strange heart-sinking feeling. Had he seen Fenrig somewhere before?

Requesting them all to follow, Philippe led them hastily to the town square, on one side of which was an imposing building.

"*La mairie*," Philippe explained. "Our town hall."

The humans seated at cafés around the square took no notice of the group of youngsters as they approached the building.

"Around the side." Philippe led them around the corner of the building and touched a stone in the wall, about five feet from the ground. The outline of a door appeared, Philippe uttered a charm, and the door opened.

"Upstairs, *vite!*" He ushered them inside.

At the top of the stone stairway, Philippe led them across a small room. Opening the full-length windows, they stepped onto a balcony overlooking the town square.

"From here we can see much of the town," explained Philippe.

"Pretty small town, I'd say," whispered Petros out of the corner of his mouth.

Streetlights around the town square illuminated the café areas. Looking down, Jack could see the humans sipping their drinks and chatting.

"The north gate." Philippe gestured to his right. "And over there," he pointed in the opposite direction, "we will defend the south gate."

At a distance of perhaps a hundred yards in each direction was the outline of a stone gateway. Streetlamps illuminated a small square in front of each.

"Here come the captains."

Henri and Cosmo were marching into the square. Between them strode a tall old man in a long robe, who carried a slim leather-bound book under his arm. Behind them were three members of each team. Jack recognised Oobit, Gandie and Radge.

"The man in the grey robe, he is Matthew, the referee," explained Philippe.

"Is he from Claville, then?" asked Rana. "That's not fair."

"No, he visits here now and then. They say he is over a thousand years old."

The referee held up a sceptre, and a glow lit up the whole square. Jack experienced a strange feeling he knew he'd felt before. He looked down. The hubbub of café chatter had ceased. As the sky brightened to that of a late summer's evening, Jack recalled the climb up to Falabray.

Henri and Cosmo stood facing each other, with their team-mates behind them. Matthew spoke briefly then threw the ball straight up into the air. The two captains leapt, but Cosmo got there first. Before he even landed, Oobit, Radge and Gandie had hexed the four Claville players in what was clearly a well-rehearsed strategy.

As the four ran towards the south end of the square, a group of five Claville players converged on them, each from a different line, firing hexes and charms. The four Cos-Howe men fell. A Claville player grabbed the ball and made a dash for it. Leaping over a table around which sat four human statues, he skilfully hid the ball in the long pleats of his robe. Reaching a dimly lit side street, he was lost to Jack's view.

Jack could see Radge and Oobit coming out of their hexes and making off in pursuit. Gandie, however, remained frozen to the spot. As the action moved out of sight, Philippe turned round.

"A good start for us, no?"

"You wait," said Petros confidently. "We're not beaten yet."

Despite having never been in Cos-Howe before that day, Petros felt he owed this loyalty to his older cousin, clearly a rising star in the Cos-Howe group.

"We never had to slow down time to play football in Rangie," said Jack. "There weren't any humans around, so we didn't need to. It's weird to see them like statues. I just wish we could see more of the players."

"They said we'd be able to see from here!" complained Rana.

"You can see both goals, so you know when a team's nearly there," said Lizzie. "But I haven't seen Ossian yet."

A bright flash shone to their left, and Jack saw a Cos-Howe player emerge from one street and turn into another. He was hovering swiftly above the ground, but close on his heels came two opponents. Jack saw Ossian join his teammate, turn and wave his left arm in a wide sweep. Instantly the two Claville players fell to the ground, crying out in pain. Ossian continued to follow his teammate, and play was lost to sight once more.

"They must be near the south gate by now," said Petros. "Can you see anything there?"

Rana strained to see, but she shook her head.

"I've got a telescope," said Philippe. "Do you want to try it?" He offered it to Fenrig, who hadn't moved from his position with his back against the balcony windows.

"Are you scared of heights?" asked Rana.

Fenrig didn't reply, but simply shook his head. Rana took the telescope from Philippe and trained it quickly upon the south gate.

"Nothing's happening there," she said. "Just one of their players guarding the gateway."

The youngsters could do little except try and guess where the action was. Another bright glow came from the south edge of the square, followed by a crackle of pops and howls of pain.

"Aha!" exclaimed Philippe. "Our secret weapon! A special hex, one you have not seen before."

In the town square eight Claville players surged forward in a phalanx. Flying over the statue-like humans, they moved rapidly northwards. Another series of pops (and howls of pain) followed as they encountered Cos-Howe players. Rana trained the telescope as they emerged onto the small square leading to the north gate. She watched in horror as the Claville players fired off a volley of hexes. As the hexes found their mark, the two hapless Cos-Howe defenders fell, yelling in agony. Placing the ball down on the ground, a Claville player took a short run up and thumped it through the defenceless gateway. The game was over.

Jack felt deflated. They'd come all this way, only to lose?

"I could hardly see any of it," moaned Lizzie, as they climbed down the stairs.

When they reached the foot of the stairway, Philippe leant forward and touched a stone in the wall. Moments later the six of them found themselves in the dimly-lit side street at the side of the town hall. The group started to make their way across the town square, whose human occupants remained motionless, as they had done throughout the match.

"The party is in the field." Philippe's smile told its own story.

They had hardly moved ten paces when they heard a shout. A young Shian, aged about twenty, ran into the square, followed closely by four others. Jack saw that the leader was Grulsh, but he had no time to say anything. The sound of an explosion in a side street was followed by flames that engulfed the ground floor of a house.

15
Crimes and Punishment

The five Shian raced across the square, shouting curses and threats. One drew a sceptre and fired off a bolt towards the *mairie*. A shower of stone debris fell to the ground, only narrowly missing Jack. A second fired off a bolt at a café window, which promptly shattered. Broken glass flew inside the café and out, lacerating all nearby. As Grulsh and the others reached the motionless humans by the café tables, each produced a stout stick and began to flail at human legs and arms. People toppled sideways, along with the tables and chairs, and lay motionless amongst smashed glass and crockery.

As the first table was overturned, Philippe drew out a small whistle and blew soundlessly into it. Within seconds, local Shian filled the square. They quickly surrounded Grulsh and the four others. A small stone was thrown down, there was a puff of smoke and the five figures fell back without a sound.

One of the Claville men then turned his sceptre on Jack and the others. A bolt flew from it, catching Jack on the chest and ricocheting onto Lizzie's head. Both fell instantly. Jack was so surprised that he barely registered the pain in his lungs.

"*Non!*" shouted Philippe, holding up his left palm to the Claville man.

His palm glowed orange, and the man's sceptre dropped to the ground.

"*Ce sont cinq.* There are five attackers. You have them already."

The Claville man, apologising profusely, produced a phial and sprinkled some powder over Jack and Lizzie.

"What happened?" Jack's chest hurt badly.

"He thought you were one of the hooligans," replied Philippe. "I'm sorry."

Jack saw that several local Shian had produced small jars from inside their capes and were going around the square dribbling what looked like oil onto the injured human bodies. Another ran across to the house that was on fire and directed a jet of cold air at the window. The flames died away, leaving only the smell of burning wood.

Henri stalked into the square, followed by an anxious-looking Cosmo. Striding through the crowd surrounding the motionless bodies, Henri surveyed the scene with evident distaste. He turned to his counterpart.

"Your friends, I believe?"

Cosmo indicated two of the bodies.

"Those two are not from Cos-Howe." He looked around, seeking support from the sizeable group that had collected.

"But the others are with you?" Henri pressed his point home.

"One travelled with us." Cosmo stared pointedly at Fenrig, who looked away. "The other two must have come later." Realising that he had to concede some ground, Cosmo went on, "Henri, I can't explain this. These Cos-Howe have shamed all of us. By Shian custom you have the right to punish them, but I ask that you let me take the three Cos-Howe boys back with us. They will face punishment when we get back."

"No." One of the local Shian stepped forward. "They must all be punished here, tonight."

"Let them go," Ossian shouted. "There's no real harm done, just a few bruises and broken glass."

"And let everyone know that we allow visitors to come and terrorise our town?" a local replied. "We will be the laughing stock of the country. No, they must all be kept here."

Realising that these disagreements were furthering the division between the two groups, Henri held up his hand for quiet.

"The three from Cos-Howe can go back home tonight, but I want an assurance that their punishment will fit the crime." Cosmo nodded solemnly at this. "The two others we shall punish ourselves. Bring them forward."

Cosmo indicated to Gandie and Radge to lift the two bodies upright. When they had done so, he examined their faces.

"Does anyone know who they are?" he demanded. "If anyone knows their names, they'd better tell me now."

There was silence. Jack saw that Fenrig was pointedly avoiding Cosmo's gaze. Cosmo then turned and nodded to Henri, who pointed at the two men in turn. A glow surrounded each of the bodies, which remained upright without the support of Gandie and Radge. Henri flicked his wrist, and the bodies dragged themselves backwards towards the war memorial. Throughout the match, none of the players had gone within ten yards of it. A mixture of stone and wrought iron, it was an imposing structure that commemorated the human dead from two wars.

The crowd followed on hesitantly, none wanting to draw too close to the ironwork. The two unnamed Shian continued to be dragged by some invisible force towards the monument, even as those following halted. When they had almost reached the memorial, they stopped. Henri turned to face the assembled crowd.

"For the violation of our town, and for shaming our visitors who came here in friendship, I condemn these creatures to the iron."

He threw a bolt from his sceptre that struck both bodies simultaneously. A blast of heat emanated from them, and they fell back onto the ironwork, melting into it. Petros gripped Jack's arm.

"They're trapped. They can't get out of that, not ever."

"It might happen," whispered Rana, who had watched in silent amazement. "I've heard a really powerful enchanter can break iron."

"Friends," declared Henri in a commanding voice, "let no one be in any doubt about this vile crime. None may go to help these creatures." He looked across at Cosmo. "I know that the others will be dealt with in the correct way. And now, let us go to the field. The King's Cup awaits."

He turned and strode back up the square, to where Grulsh and the other two Cos-Howe men lay motionless. Taking control of the situation, Cosmo indicated again to Radge and

Oobit to bring the bodies with them. Radge made as if to levitate the bodies, but Cosmo shook his head.

"No. We'll drag them."

Waving his sceptre, he produced three long ropes. Slowly they dragged the bodies across to the side of the square. Heads and shoulders bumped defencelessly over kerbstones and hit the sides of tables, scratches and grazes began to appear and blood started to trail from Grulsh's head. Seeing that this public display was meant to placate him, Henri simply nodded and turned into the street that led to the gate. The light in the sky diminished, and the humans who had been frozen in position began to move again. A few started to massage their arms and legs, and there were exclamations about the smashed window and upturned tables. Accusations were thrown, and quickly denied.

"This is not good." Philippe had stopped with Jack. "There will be many arguments tonight. Tomorrow when it is light, they will start searching. That means trouble."

Jack, remembering the hex that had caught him, didn't know how to reply, and instead hastened to catch up with Petros and the others.

Within minutes, the Shian had reached the field outside the town. Cosmo, Oobit and Radge, breathing heavily, released their grip on the ropes, leaving Grulsh and the other two bodies motionless. Fenrig ran up, but stopped as he saw Grulsh's inert body, blood trickling from one of his ears. Sullenly Fenrig turned away and sat down by the wall.

Matthew the referee stood in front of the fiery cup, which still glowed, suspended in mid-air. He glanced at Cosmo, and there was a formal nod of the head before he turned to address the crowd.

"My friends," said Matthew, "we thank you for coming tonight. I know that your friendship, which goes back for so long, is what matters. Tonight's unfortunate events will not mar that. The King's Cup is awarded to the captain of Claville."

Henri strode forward and made as if to grab the fiery chalice. As his hands touched the flames they disappeared, leaving only a momentary wisp of smoke in their place. A loud laugh greeted this display. Jack saw that as the flames disappeared, so too did Matthew.

"To our friendship!" shouted Henri.

The party quickly kicked in, and even the despondent Cos-Howe players were soon eating and drinking heartily and regaling each other with incidents from the game. Jack and Petros sat down, each sipping a cup of juniper juice. Looking up, Jack saw Fenrig, his back to them, talking earnestly with a tall Shian Jack had an uncomfortable feeling he'd seen before. The hairs on the back of his neck were bristling, and a wave of nausea passed through him. Then Fenrig turned round and looked at Jack, a cold, contemptuous stare that made Jack's stomach churn. He nudged Petros.

"What is it?"

"It's Fenrig, he was up at Falabray, with the Brashat. That other guy was there too."

Petros looked at Jack. He didn't need to ask if he was sure. The answer was in his eyes.

"It's time we were going, then. You get Rana and Lizzie. I'll find Ossian."

Blushing and giggling, the girls were standing next to one of the Claville players, a strong lad of about sixteen. Paying the

French player no notice, Jack urgently whispered, "We need to go. We're leaving now."

"But we're having fun!" protested Lizzie. "I don't want to go."

Jack wondered how it was that Lizzie managed to change her mind so completely when it suited her.

"Ossian's not pleased at being dragged away from the party," said Petros, who had returned. "He's found a French girl."

Keeping an eye out for Fenrig and the tall Brashat, Jack quickly found Ossian and told him that they would be taking two horses whether he, Ossian, came with them or not. Reluctantly, Ossian followed Jack back to the others.

"Just let me tell Cosmo," he explained. "I'll have to make sure the horses are all right."

Frustratingly, Ossian took some time accomplishing this simple task. Cosmo returned with him and expressed his thanks for their support.

"Well, Jack, you didn't bring us the victory tonight. Do you play yourself?"

Jack nodded. "I'm fast."

"Maybe next year we'll give you a try-out."

He made as if to leave, then turned back.

"What you witnessed tonight in the square. I hope you'll have the good sense not to broadcast it. We'll deal with it ourselves, all right? And I'll see that Grulsh's cousin gets back."

"We'll take the same horses," stated Ossian bluntly.

Without delay, they mounted and started to canter across the field. Though tired, Jack gripped his cousin's belt tightly. As they reached galloping pace, Ossian cried, "Horse and hattock!" and the horses rose swiftly into the air.

★ ★ ★

Once Ossian had stabled the two horses, he rejoined the others.

"I suppose I'll have to make sure you all get back safely," he grumbled as he led them around Arthur's Seat.

Jack saw that they were near the foot of St Margaret's Street.

"I know this street," he said. "The castle's up and along to the left."

"I'm still takin' you back. I don't want you gettin' lost."

The small group made their way in silence onto the esplanade.

"You lot can get back from here," said Ossian sullenly. "I'll take the low road from Cos-Howe."

"Aren't you coming in with us?" demanded Rana. "You can take the low road from under the castle."

"No chance!" Without any further word, Ossian turned and ran off down the road.

Petros organised the four of them into a huddle, and within seconds they were in the Shian square. Jack saw that a light still showed in their house, and glanced nervously at Petros. They had no time to discuss how to get indoors quietly, for just then Uncle Doonya appeared at the front door. He stood silently, staring hard, his jaw clenched.

The youngsters stopped, uncertain what to do next. The decision was taken for them as Grandpa Sandy emerged. He whispered something to Doonya, who took one long hard look before going back inside. Grandpa wordlessly beckoned them in. As they reached the door he said, "It's late. We'll discuss this tomorrow. Up to bed, all of you."

16
The Tailor's Apprentice

Jack woke with a start.

"Come on, time to get up." Petros was shaking him by the arm.

Jack forced his eyes open, but that was too much effort.

I've only just got to sleep.

Petros shook his shoulder roughly, and this time Jack forced himself out of bed. Dressing hurriedly, he followed Petros downstairs. Aunt Katie pushed a bowl of porridge towards him as he came into the kitchen.

"You'd better get this down you," she said kindly. "You have to be at Gilmore's in ten minutes."

Petros opened the front door.

"Your dad wants to speak to you later," she continued as Petros slouched off, but he was already through the door, and if he heard he didn't show any sign of it.

Katie turned to Jack and was about to speak, then seemed to think better of it. After a pause, she said simply, "Try and stay awake. A big day today."

Her mouth was smiling, but Jack thought that her eyes were not really joining in.

"Don't forget your lunch." Katie held forward a small packet and a satchel.

Jack trudged along the bright square towards Gilmore's house. He would have given anything to go back to bed – he really didn't want to do this. And to think how excited he'd been all year about becoming an apprentice! That meant you weren't a child any more, and learning to be a tailor would open up all sorts of magycks to him. But even this prospect was not enough to cheer Jack up this morning. The best he could do was console himself that he didn't have to face his uncle just yet.

Turning into the small garden in front of the tailor's house, he saw to his astonishment that Fenrig was standing there. The front door opened, and a small, wizened man emerged.

"Come in, come in," he said matter-of-factly. "The others are through the back."

They followed him through to the small workshop. A wooden table ran almost the length of the room, and shelves along the back wall all but groaned under the weight of cloth. Entering, Jack saw two Shian youngsters already hard at work.

"Hiya, Jack," called Freya. "Ready for your first day? Who's your friend?"

Jack smiled back, but wasn't sure how to answer either question. Freya was sitting halfway along the long table, sewing two pieces of cloth together with a silken thread.

"Sit down, sit down," fussed Gilmore, ushering them towards two stools at the far end. "Now, firstly you need to know who's who. That's Freya there. Her mother is a very talented seamstress. And that's Doxer. You won't get much out of him. He's been here a year, and I've yet to hear him utter more than a few words."

"Now then," he continued, "who can tell me why we need tailors?"

Jack looked across at Fenrig, who rolled his eyes to the ceiling.

"To make clothes?" said Jack, feeling that some answer – even a banal one – was required.

"But what sort?" pressed Gilmore. "Don't tell me nobody's told you about special clothes."

"Clothes so we can make ourselves invisible and play tricks on humans," said Fenrig, deciding to break his silence.

"That's not the first thing I would have said," stated Gilmore flatly. "We can make all sorts of special clothes, for many different occasions: to make ourselves invisible, or smaller, or able to fly. We can also make special bandages for a host of injuries." His eyes twinkled. "Now, you may be tempted to try out some of the clothes you make here on humans outside, but that is strictly forbidden. We have to live with humans all around us outside; making fun of those poor creatures is not permitted."

He indicated two small piles of cloths on the table.

"Take one pile each, and tell me what you can of each cloth."

"I thought we were here to learn how to make charmed clothes," complained Fenrig.

"First, you have to know about the cloth," replied Gilmore gruffly.

He left the new apprentices to their respective piles and went to help Doxer. Fenrig muttered under his breath as he rummaged half-heartedly through his pile. Though exhausted, Jack thought he'd better make the most of it. There were twelve pieces of cloth, all different: some feather-light, others rough and coarse; some non-descript, others silk-like and distinctive. Jack knew he was well below par this morning, but still wasn't sure what to do. After a few moments, Gilmore returned.

"Well, what can you tell me? Fenrig, you first."

Fenrig waved his hand over the pile of cloths. "They're cloths. That one's green. So's that one. That one's wool. Dunno what *they* are."

Gilmore made little effort to hide his disappointment at this unenthusiastic attempt.

"I hope that you, Jack, can do a little better?"

Jack started to describe the cloths in front of him, naming colours, textures and possible materials. He had almost finished when Gilmore said, "But what can you tell me about their uses?" Then, seeing the lack of comprehension on both boys' faces, he continued, "This one here is a bandage used to heal someone who's been bitten by a werewolf. That purple one can make even a hideous Shian appear attractive – to a human. And that one there can make you invisible."

Freya looked up at Jack and smiled knowingly. Even Doxer, as silent as ever, was grinning.

"I hope now you see that there's a lot more to a piece of cloth than its colour or texture. Now, we'll spend the rest of today learning what makes these pieces special."

To Jack's surprise, the morning went quickly. Gilmore's enthusiasm was infectious enough to keep him awake, even if he wasn't on top form. When it came to lunchtime, he was grateful when Freya beckoned him over. Fenrig pushed past him wordlessly, and left the workshop.

"I should've realised that was Fenrig. I heard yesterday that he'd moved into the square. He's in the house at the end," Freya added, seeing Jack's puzzled look. "The empty house, remember? The one with the low road entrance. D'you know him?"

"He was at Falabray, with the Brashat. And he was in France yesterday . . ." Jack's voice tailed off.

"It's all right, I'll hear soon enough." Freya seemed to understand that Jack didn't want to say more for the moment.

They shared their lunch, and Freya filled Jack in on some of the ins and outs of being a tailor's apprentice. When he restarted work for the afternoon, Jack was grateful to see that Fenrig did not return from his lunch break, and he spent a quiet afternoon being shown how to arrange and store the different types of cloth.

"A good start, I think," said Gilmore happily, when three o'clock came. "I'm sure your friend will feel better tomorrow."

Jack made his way silently to the door. Gilmore, carefully examining some silken threads, did not see Freya as she winked at Jack and held her forefinger to her lips. Nonplussed, Jack watched as she laid a small piece of black cloth on the table, waved her left hand over it and whispered something. The cloth sparkled briefly, then rose and hovered for a few moments before coming to rest on the table. Freya grinned with satisfaction, but indicated for Jack to go before Gilmore realised what was happening.

Waving goodbye, Jack made his way to the door. Doxer nodded silently as he passed him and continued to work away at a piece of cloth on the table. Jack had the strange feeling of being watched as he opened the door, but when he looked back, Doxer was still staring fixedly at the table.

17
Facing the Music

Jack dawdled, hoping Petros would get home first and draw some of his uncle's anger. As he entered the house, he heard Rana and Lizzie playing in the front room. Cautiously opening the door, he peered in.

"Hi, Jack! How'd your first day go?"

Jack looked nervously behind him, not sure who else was in the house.

"It's all right," continued Rana. "Dad's gone out with Mum. We got an earful this morning, but Lizzie told them how Ossian didn't tell us how we could get back, so it was really his fault. They were more worried than angry. Grandpa was OK."

When Petros came in, Rana took great pleasure in telling him that he was only safe until their father returned. After Lizzie had reassured him somewhat, the four cousins sat and discussed their encounter with Tamlina and their travels. The day before had been very full, and both boys could have done with a slow day to recover. Rana and Lizzie had been luckier, with only an hour of tuition from their mother to distract them from play. Jack gave a start as he saw the door open and his uncle and grandfather standing in the doorway. The happy chatter stilled instantly.

Grandpa put his hand on Doonya's shoulder and said, "I think we could all do with a chat." He walked in and sat down. Doonya remained standing in the doorway and glowered silently.

"Now, you all know that you should have come straight home from Keldy yesterday." Grandpa spoke evenly. "Petros, I thought we could rely on you. You're not a child anymore."

"But Ossian took us to Cos-Howe, and we didn't know how to get back from there," protested Petros.

"You should still have come home by evening. Staying out so late could be very dangerous. Going all the way to France was reckless. And we heard what went on in Claville — a bad business. Shian have to live alongside humans — there and here." Grandpa spoke evenly, without raising his voice. Doonya, still standing in the doorway, clenched his jaw.

"We've not let Jack far out of our sight. I dread to think what might have happened if you'd met any Brashat."

"But we did," blurted out Jack. "One of the Brashat boys was in France, and he's started work with Gilmore today. After the match I saw another one that I'm sure was at Falabray."

"Do you mean you were with Brashat last night?!" Doonya exclaimed. "Well, that just proves how dangerous it is to go off by yourselves. You know what they did at midsummer. That fire you saw wasn't the only one. It's a miracle no one was killed."

"I'm sorry, Dad," said Petros. "I know we should've been home earlier, but we did send a grig from Cos-Howe. It just seemed a good opportunity to see somewhere different. And we really didn't know how to get back."

"The Brashat boy," said Grandpa to Jack. "Is he about your age, with dark hair?"

Jack nodded. "He's called Fenrig. I'm sure he was at Falabray. His cousin's one of the Cos-Howe men."

"Atholmor is allowing this Brashat boy to start his apprenticeship here." Grandpa sounded wearied. "He's moved into the house at the foot of the square with Mawkit. Atholmor must have his reasons, although it's hard to understand them. The Brashat don't like the cities – they hate the humans too much. If they're moving here, that spells trouble."

"We'll need to discuss this with the Congress," stated Doonya firmly. "For the time being, none of you is to go out from the square without an adult, is that clear?"

"You mean, we can't go out to the High Street?" wailed Rana.

"It's for your own safety," replied her father. "I don't believe for a minute that he's really here as an apprentice, that just doesn't make sense. Jack, you keep a close watch on him. If he's a real Brashat he'll be a nasty piece of work."

"Jack," continued Grandpa, "I think for the time being you'll have to stay under the castle."

"Why are they allowed out and I have to stay here?" complained Jack. "That's not fair."

"We'll see in a while how things are. Two weeks, anyway. After that you'll all be starting your lessons with Murkle and Daid."

Jack scowled. *Stay under here for a fortnight?! How boring is that?*

"Cheer up, Jack. I know it's upsetting, but it's for your own good. So, tell me how you got on today at Gilmore's. He's one of the finest tailors in the country. You'll learn a lot from him."

Sullenly, Jack recounted his day in the tailor's workshop. He had to repeat the same story when Aunt Katie came in later, but at least the recriminations concerning the previous day seemed to be over. The new perceived danger of a Brashat boy in the Shian square had downgraded such concerns.

Over the next two weeks Jack continued to go to Gilmore's workshop, and his life settled down into a steady, if dull, pattern. Learning about different cloths, in truth, was a bit monotonous, and he looked forward to the time when he would be making special clothes.

Fenrig appeared each day but was often late, and always uncommunicative. At three each day he seemed to disappear. Jack never saw him in the square, and Mawkit's house seemed deserted. If Grandpa had learned Atholmor's reasons for allowing Fenrig to be there, he wasn't letting on.

A message from Keldy revealed that Ossian had been grounded for a month. Neither Jack nor Petros felt comfortable making contact with anyone from Cos-Howe, and so no news was forthcoming about the fate of Grulsh and the two others brought back from France. Jack thought of asking Fenrig, but didn't know how to broach the subject, and Fenrig made it clear that he didn't want to talk in any case.

The two weeks of Jack's enforced stay under the castle passed slowly. He was desperate to get out into the fresh air again. He had enjoyed being out among the humans, too. He couldn't understand Ossian's antagonism towards humans and had been looking forward to watching them closely with his cousins. Now he would have to learn about them from Daid the tutor.

18
Shian Tales ...

Two weeks after the Claville match, Jack and the other new apprentices met formally together for their new lessons. Apart from Fenrig, there was Boyce, who had joined Petros in working with Cormac the woodcarver; Lee-Brog, apprentice to Tramen the shoemaker; Purdy from next door, who was learning to be a baker; Séan, who had joined Nachie the bard; and Kaol, who was learning music with Arvin. From outside the castle came Suque, who helped with the horses, and Diana, who was apprentice to a huntsman.

The youngsters had all finished work at twelve instead of three on the Monday and now congregated outside Murkle's house for lessons in Shian tales. However, none was bold enough to approach the door.

"He's really bad-tempered," said Boyce. "Petros said his lessons are awful. He just drones on and on."

"I heard he uses his belt," said Suque. "Well, if he beats me, I've got a horsewhip, and I'll . . ." Her voice trailed off.

"You the one with the mad mother who ran away?" Boyce sneered at Jack.

Jack, turning beetroot, stammered, "Sh—She's not mad. She's . . . highly strung."

A derisive snort revealed Boyce's opinion of this. There was a strained silence for a few moments.

"I don't see why you lot are waiting," said Fenrig, who had just arrived. Striding up, he knocked firmly on the door. The sound echoed through the house, but there was no answer.

"If he's no' in, we can have the afternoon off," said Séan hopefully.

Fenrig knocked again. "Murkle knows more tales than anyone else this far south," he said without turning round. "It's got to be better than sorting out handkerchief rejects, anyway."

If Murkle knows so much, maybe he can tell us about the King's Cup, thought Jack.

A bolt was pulled creakily back. The door opened slowly to reveal a tall, dishevelled man. Under a long and grimy black cloak, his trouser ends were visibly frayed, his shirt was similarly worn and his gloves fingerless.

"What is it? What do you want?" he asked in a loud voice.

"We've come for our lesson," said Fenrig equally loudly.

"What?" He cupped his hand to his ear.

"Our lesson," shouted Fenrig.

"Ah, the lesson." He didn't sound very enthusiastic. "You'd better come in."

The hallway led into a small gloomy front room containing five chairs and two tables, arranged in front of a bare fireplace.

A melancholy portrait stared from the one picture to grace the dank walls, but the room's most overpowering sensation was its smell, like stale over-boiled cabbage. Jack curled his lip in distaste.

He hasn't even bothered to get the lumis crystals working again. Cheapskate.

As the new apprentices tried to crowd inside, Murkle looked around with dismay.

"Oh no, no, this won't do. Out again, the lot of you."

With difficulty, the nine extricated themselves from the room, some stepping outside the house, others turning and going into the small rear kitchen. Murkle grabbed Suque, the last to leave, as she was in the doorway. Without explanation, he placed his right hand on her head and clicked the fingers of his left hand. He whispered inaudibly, and she instantly shrank to half her usual height, whereupon he nudged her back into the room. Suque squealed in surprise, but realising what had happened, she went and climbed up onto one of the now towering chairs. The others followed in turn and were soon squeezed up onto four chairs.

"Let's get started," announced Murkle. Remaining at his usual height, he loomed above the apprentices. "Now, the Congress has decided that you all need to be taught Shian tales and human lessons. I can't speak for human beings, having no contact with them if I can help it," at this point Fenrig smirked, "but why you can't learn Shian tales at home with your parents I don't know."

"He's going to be a bundle of laughs," whispered Séan to Jack.

"I am not a bundle of anything," snapped Murkle, whose hearing seemed to have improved dramatically. Several of the youngsters exchanged nervous glances.

"My unpleasant task is to impart to you impertinent young things some of my knowledge of Shian folklore," he continued. "I warn you that I do not tolerate insolence or bad behaviour. We will start with the tale of the giant and the troll. Many years ago ..." Murkle paused as he saw a hand shoot up.

"Please, Murkle," said Purdy brightly, "I know this story. It happened hundreds of years ago, and this giant ..." Her voice trailed off as she saw the look of dislike on the teacher's face.

"I did not ask if any of you knew this story already," he barked. "And, as far as I am aware, the Congress has not asked you to teach the new apprentices. Or perhaps I'm mistaken, perhaps you are indeed the new teacher. Well, young Purdy, I'm obviously wasting my time here. Why don't you take over?" He sneered sarcastically as she squirmed in embarrassment.

"Does anyone else want to be the teacher?" asked Murkle, glaring round at the others.

Jack, like everyone else, had suddenly found the floor very interesting. *I'm not asking him about the King's Cup – or anything else.*

After a pause, Murkle resumed.

"The giant lived in a cave, far away to the north. In those days there were giants living on most hillsides, but they always lived alone ..."

His monotonous voice lacked even the barest inflection to make it interesting. For two hours he spoke without stopping. There was no obvious connection between the tales, and no discussion about what each had signified. He paused only once, to summon a small goblet of water, which he quickly drained.

By three o'clock, the apprentices were all in a state of torpor. Boyce had twice dozed off, his head sliding down onto Jack's shoulder, whereupon Jack had nudged him sharply in the ribs. Murkle drew his final story to a close, and for the first time since he had started, he looked round at his audience.

"Next Monday we will continue with tales of the north countries. In time, I intend to discuss demons, including Amadan. I will expect you to be on time." He stood up and walked to the door.

Diana, first to her feet, strode to the doorway. Murkle bent down and placed his hand unceremoniously on her head, and whispered under his breath. In a second, she had regained her normal height, and she left without a word. The others quickly jumped off their chairs and formed a line.

Within a minute they were all outside. After the gloominess of Murkle's front room, the square seemed very bright. Fenrig immediately ran to the foot of the square, but the others remained where they were.

Jack inhaled deeply and savoured the fresh air that came from the warren pipes in the rock wall.

"Well, that was a waste of time," announced Boyce. "If I'd wanted a good sleep I could've just gone back to bed."

"You mean we have to go through that every week?" moaned Kaol. "What's the Congress think they're doing, making him a teacher?"

Jack and Purdy strolled along the square, and she turned into the path leading up to her door.

"See you later."

Jack smiled back, and walked onto the next house. Aunt Katie called him through from the kitchen.

"How did you get on today, Jack dear?" she asked brightly.

Jack mumbled something about getting on all right, but Katie wasn't giving up that easily.

"Come on, I know you're getting on well at Gilmore's, but tell me what this afternoon was like."

Jack really wasn't in the mood to discuss his day, but his aunt persisted.

"It's boring, all right?" he snapped. "He just droned on and on. He even made the good stories boring."

Though taken aback at Jack's anger, Aunt Katie rallied. "Well, we had heard that he's not very exciting," she admitted. "But the stories must be good, and he knows ever so many. That's why he was chosen to be your teacher. Never mind, you've got Daid on Thursday. I'm sure he'll convince you that we can all learn a lot from the humans."

Jack knew his aunt meant well, but he just wasn't in the mood. How could someone who knew so many good tales be so uninspiring? If human lessons were anything like the Shian tales, two afternoons a week might as well be written off, and there was still no word of him being allowed out beyond the Shian square. If he didn't get out and about soon, he'd go mad.

19
. . . and Human Lessons

On Thursday afternoon, the new apprentices met outside Daid's house. Next door to Murkle's, it was on the face of it very similar. As Purdy was about to knock, the door opened, and they were greeted by a jovial man who ushered them in. A broad smile almost reached both ears, and his eyes shone with good humour.

The apprentices trooped into the front room, as they had done in Murkle's house, and it was immediately obvious that the two were strikingly different. Whereas Murkle's front room had been drab and cramped, Daid's was bright and roomy, even if the hundreds of books ranged haphazardly on shelves did make it look untidy. Lumis crystals in the outer wall caught the light from the square outside and diffused it around the room. There were enough chairs for everyone, and in the corner stood an upright piano.

"I've fixed the room so that it will accommodate us all," chortled Daid. "Make yourselves comfortable."

He began to tell stories about human life and history: some sad, some funny. Jack and most of the class sat enthralled – Daid was clearly an accomplished storyteller.

"Humans are stupid," said Fenrig after a while, interrupting Daid mid-sentence. "They think they're clever, but they're not."

"Now, what makes you think that, young man? I grant you, there are stupid ones, but are they any worse than us?"

"My dad says we should get them whenever we can," continued Fenrig, not in the least abashed at Daid's response.

"Well now, that would be unfortunate," said Daid with a smile. "We have to live near humans, if not with them. Does it profit us to be hostile?"

"We're getting them back for all they've done to Shian down the years," said Boyce.

"It's true that in the past humans did some terrible things to Shian," conceded Daid. "To illustrate, I'll show you a simulacrum."

Jack watched as Daid used his sceptre to project the simulacrum onto the wall.

Just like Grandpa did.

Great crowds and burning houses; people tied to wooden stakes and set on fire. Others throttled and left to hang from trees, or tied to rocks and thrown into rivers. Silent screams of terror and pain shouted out from the wall, an eerie soundless echo of past torments. Purdy shuddered.

"Things got very bad after the Stone was taken away, as you can see. Weak without the Stone's power, we withdrew, away from the towns. Long ago the humans had all sorts of names for the Shian: some good, like the 'good neighbours'; some bad, like the 'demons'. Well, it got so bad that eventually they only thought of us as demons. And there are demons, such as Amadan, whose touch alone can kill. Both sides committed vile crimes."

"Whole Shian families died out, didn't they?" asked Suque.

"That's right. Then someone had the bright idea of teaching humans that the Shian were nothing more than garden sprites, creatures no more powerful than lacewing flies. That ruse saved us."

"But that sounds like a grig," stated Diana.

"Exactly. And humans barely notice them. So, who can tell me about their dealings with humans?"

"I like using paving hexes so they trip up," proclaimed Boyce.

"That's kids' stuff," snorted Fenrig. "I bet you've never kidnapped a human, or put them to work in the forges."

"And why do you like picking on humans?" asked Daid tolerantly.

"Because they're there and I feel like it."

"A rather unimaginative impulse, I should say. Now, don't get the impression that I believe humans to be off limits. The haughty, the mean-spirited, they all deserve to be taken down a peg or two. Kidnapping – well, the Seelie do not approve of that. You know some good humans have Shian guardian angels, though they seldom realise it."

Suque raised her hand. "Who should we play tricks on, then?"

"A good question, young lady. To answer, we need to find out more about what makes humans tick. Now, who has read any human books?"

Purdy put up her hand. "My mother showed me a book about baking. Humans use funny flour; their food tastes awful."

Maybe that's why Aunt Katie's such a lousy cook, thought Jack. *She's half-human.*

"I'm sure we all know that human food can be disgusting, but I meant human books about humans. They tell stories, just like us. Histories, novels and plays that let us see what makes humans what they are."

"You mean stupid and greedy?" asked Fenrig, at which there was a muffled giggle around the room.

"No more so than some of the best known Shian characters from our own history," said Daid without rising to the bait. "Now, I want you all to choose one book from my shelves over there, it doesn't matter which one. Over the next few weeks, one at a time, I want you to come back and tell us all about the book you've chosen, and what it tells us about humans. Is that clear?"

Fenrig was first up. Without looking, he grabbed the book at the end of the shelf and strutted out. The others followed more slowly, taking time to look at two or three books before selecting one. As they all stood on the pavement outside, Jack glanced at the book Purdy had taken.

"A Victorian Lady's Highland Journal?" he asked. "What's that about?"

"I don't know. I liked the look of it. What's yours?"

"*A History of the English-Speaking Peoples, Volume Three.* All the short ones were gone by the time I got to choose. Are you going home?"

"Yes. Mum said she wanted to ask me about everything as soon as we finished today."

The next week the youngsters gathered in Daid's front room. Purdy was not there due to illness – a case, her mother said, of having eaten some human sweets found by Rana. The others found a seat each and brought out their books, with the exception of Fenrig.

"Lost it," he said carelessly when questioned by Daid.

"Lost it?! These books are valuable, I entrusted them to you. Which one did you take?"

"Dunno. *Candid*, something like that."

"That is a classic tale, which will help us all to learn about the human condition. I hope you will be able to locate it later today?"

"Or what?" sneered Fenrig. "You mean you'll stop me from learning about Dameves?"

"These lessons are not optional, young man," said Daid through gritted teeth, the previous week's easy-going manner having deserted him. "You *will* find that book and bring it back to me by tomorrow evening. Otherwise I dare say the Congress will review your place here."

"My dad knows Amadan. You wouldn't want *him* to get involved, would you?" said Fenrig sullenly.

Daid stiffened for a moment, then decided to let pass what was undoubtedly an empty threat.

"I trust the rest of you have taken better care of your books?" he asked evenly. "You, Boyce. Which book did you take?"

"It was a play set in Italy," answered Boyce. "It's called *Romeo and Juliet*, but it was confusing. I didn't recognise a lot of the words."

"That's excusable. It was written a long time ago, when human speech was rather different. Can you tell us what the story was about?"

"Well, these two young people are in love," began Boyce, at which point Jack and several of the others began making mooning kissing faces at him. He snarled, annoyed by the teasing, but continued to narrate the basic plot.

"Very good," said Daid, when Boyce had finished. "Now, who can tell me why this story is important?"

"Because it shows humans are capable of loving," answered Diana.

"It shows they can't deal with love, you mean," retorted Séan. "Fighting each other, all because two people want to be together."

"Just like the Shian, in other words," said Daid, at which there was a moment of silence, broken only by Fenrig's derisive snort. "Perhaps you could tell me, young Fenrig, what it is about humans that so antagonises you?"

Fenrig stared back at the tutor, and there was a pause before he said simply, "Shian and humans shouldn't mix."

"Do you mean never mix, or only when a Shian needs something that only a human has?"

"They've got nothing we need," answered Fenrig. "They think they have all the answers, but if they're so clever, how come they only live seventy or eighty years?"

"Ah, now that is an interesting point, and it will take some time to discuss. Who can tell me . . ." Daid's voice trailed off as a large figure appeared at the window, causing the room to darken appreciably. Jack turned, but could only make out an indistinct face.

"That's all for today," said Daid hurriedly. "Next week you're all to bring me a story about human nature. Ask your parents, or anyone. True story or false, it doesn't matter. Now, come on, out with you."

Flustered, Daid ushered the youngsters out of the house. As Jack and the others began to walk away, they saw someone emerge from the side of the house and slip quietly in at the front door.

Without preamble, Boyce walked up to Jack and punched him on the side of the head, knocking him to the ground.

"That's for *kissy kissy,*" he snarled.

Surprised by the attack, Jack sat for a moment. *I'll get you for that*, he thought. *Not now, when there's no one else around.*

"Who was that at the window?" asked Diana. "Daid looked frightened."

"Probably one of his human friends," snorted Fenrig.

"Humans are too big to come under the castle," said Purdy.

"Wouldn't they shrink down, same as us?" queried Suque.

"That gate doesn't work on humans – Dad told me," said Purdy.

"I saw a face, but not very clearly," said Jack, getting to his feet. "It was an old man. I think he had a scar on his cheek."

"Who are you going to ask for your story, Jack?" asked Purdy.

"My Aunt Katie," replied Jack. "Her dad was a human, so she's got loads of stories." Jack paused, then, out of devilment, he asked, "What about you, Fenrig?"

"I'm not wasting my time on that," snapped Fenrig, and he raced off.

Jack saw him go round to the back of Mawkit's house, and thought of following to see exactly where he went, but then realised that this was futile. Fenrig had perfected the art of making himself scarce. Jack knew that he wouldn't see him again until the next morning.

20
The Aximon

As predicted, Fenrig appeared at the workshop the next day, and every other working day over the next few weeks. Their routine had settled down, and while there was no warmth in their relationship, each tolerated the other. Jack tried hard to get to grips with his work, and occasionally showed some promise. Fenrig, meanwhile, continued to gripe about not being allowed to make charmed clothes.

If tailoring was becoming routine, so were Murkle's lessons. These remained as uninteresting as on the first afternoon. Daid's lessons, on the other hand, were a mixture of delight and frustration. Sometimes he brimmed over with eagerness, keen to tell stories or impart little nuggets of information. At other times, he seemed anxious or preoccupied, unable to concentrate on the thread of a conversation.

Jack found that Aunt Katie was more than ready to talk about humans and their strange ways, although there were moments when she became sad when talking about her father and his human family. Jack found this inexplicable, and after a lesson at Daid's he quizzed her about this.

"Aunt Katie, why's it so hard to talk about your dad?"

"Oh, it's just that he's not here anymore. He left his family to come and live among the Shian, but you know that humans don't live that long."

"How old was he when he died?"

"He was sixty – not especially young. But they have a different way of dealing with death. His family accepted his decision to leave, even though they knew it would change him. When he died we let them know. They just said he had gone to a better place."

"Where?"

"Oh, it's not a real place," said Katie, getting flustered.

"Is it one of the secrets about death that the King's Cup is supposed to tell us?"

"Now, Jack, that's enough about that. It's time you were getting outside. Go and see what the others are doing."

"But Aunt—" Jack's voice trailed off as he saw his aunt start to cry again. He left her and went outside. Petros was by the grocery shop at the top end of the square, and called out as he saw Jack approach. "What's up?" he said.

"Your mum's upset. I asked about her father. You know, for our lessons with Daid. She gets so far, and then she just starts crying."

"She's always been like that. Listen, I was speaking to Dad earlier on, and he says that he'll teach us a hex so you can come up above the castle again."

Jack's eyes lit up. It seemed like forever since he'd been out in the open. His two-week ban had been indefinitely extended – proof, claimed Petros, that the Congress was divided about having a Brashat under the castle. Jack could hardly wait.

"Where's your dad? Can we see him now?"

"After supper. You won't be allowed out on your own, but it's OK to come with me. That way there's someone around in case anyone tries to get you."

"How many hexes d'you know?" asked Jack.

"A few. They're not very strong, though. I think Dad's going to teach us something better. But you know the rules: hexes are a last resort."

"The players in Claville used hexes," pointed out Jack. "That was just part of the game."

"The bad ones aren't allowed in sport. Remember Rob's hex in the wrestling match? He was in trouble for that. Sport hexes will hurt you, but they don't last long. And you're not allowed to use them against children."

If I get a good one, I'm using it on Boyce, thought Jack as they headed back to the house.

That evening, Doonya took Petros and Jack aside.

"I know you want to get outside the square, Jack. Well, things have settled down now. The Brashat have been quiet, and no one's tried to get near the Stone. Fenrig doesn't seem to have any particular interest in you, and that's good, or else he's a very poor kind of spy. And remember his friends who took him to France? Well, they've been taken care of."

"Fenrig was muttering about a binding hex. What's that?" asked Jack.

"It holds someone, as if they're frozen, only without being frozen. It's not like being suspended. I've heard they'll be kept that way for a long time. Cosmo had no option, considering what happened to the others in Claville."

"Putting them to the iron was a bit much for what they did, wasn't it?" asked Petros.

"The Claville Shian have good ties with the humans. Grulsh and the others violated their sense of what's right. They're out of the way, but there may be others, so don't get careless. It's all right for you to go out, as long as you're accompanied, and as long as you know how to look after yourself."

Jack nodded eagerly.

"We've taught you some simple hexes, but you know the rules. If you cast a hex maliciously, it'll return to you three times over. If it's very serious, then the Congress may have to be told, and then you'll really be in trouble. Got that?"

Both youngsters indicated that they understood, but Jack was only half-listening. Everyone knew that you couldn't go around hexing people. He just wished Uncle Doonya would get on with it.

"Whenever you go out, take these Aximon figures Cormac's made," continued Doonya. "Don't stray too far. If anyone attacks you, grip the figure in your right hand and say, 'Salvus!' three times. That will slow down your attacker and give you time to get away – but only if you really believe it. You can't fool the Aximon."

Jack examined one of the figures in detail.

"How's it work?"

"It's a mixture hex," replied Doonya. "Part Shian, part human. Because of that, the Brashat won't use them. It'll disarm an attacker, but only briefly. Look after the figures. If they save your skins, they'll be priceless. And remember to say the words."

"Yes, Dad," said Petros, and Jack nodded in agreement.

"And Petros." Doonya looked sternly at his son. "Don't think I don't know about some of the tricks you get up to with the humans. Don't go overboard, all right? And don't draw attention to yourself."

"Is it only the Brashat I have to worry about?" asked Jack.

"It's anyone who might try to grab you," replied Doonya. "Because of our history with them, the Brashat are the most likely. Tomorrow you can go out again. But take care."

Jack found it hard to get to sleep that night, and all through the next morning at Gilmore's, though tired, he was impatient for leaving time. When Gilmore finally said the apprentices could finish, for once it was Jack who was fastest out the door, leaving Fenrig and Freya looking bewildered. Doxer, as usual, was impassive.

21
The Spiral Trinity

Jack hesitated when he stepped onto the esplanade. It wasn't busy, but something made him hang back. How far should he go? He might have Shian enemies – but what about the humans? Were any of them dangerous? As he and Petros strolled around the esplanade, they chatted about Shian-human tensions.

"Ossian really doesn't like humans, does he?" said Jack. "All that stuff about Dameves."

"He's all right. Most of that's just show. I bet he didn't tell you Uncle Hart's a guardian for a human near Keldy. Ossian helps his dad out with that. You've got to take him with a pinch of salt."

"What about the Aximon figure?" asked Jack. "I still don't understand what your dad meant about it being a mixture hex."

"I'm not sure. I heard Dad and Grandpa talking about hexes late one night. I'd gone downstairs for a drink. Then they talked about ghosts and a prophecy, but I couldn't hear much of what they said. It's about the Stone, and they mentioned a cup too, and there was something called Gosol. They seemed pretty excited by it."

"You don't think it was the King's Cup, do you?" said Jack. "Grandpa told me that was just a story Shian told themselves about their power returning one day."

"Dad said it disappeared ages back. We could ask him. He's calmed down now about us going to France."

Eventually, the desire to find out overcame Jack's relief at being allowed out again, and the pair returned to the Shian square. They found Doonya, Grandpa Sandy and Aunt Katie talking in the kitchen, but the conversation died as Jack and Petros entered. Six inquisitive eyes faced the boys as they stood in the doorway. Sensing that they had intruded, Jack said, "Is there any juniper juice?"

Aunt Katie wordlessly poured two cups from a large jug and pushed them towards the youngsters.

"Thanks, Mum," said Petros, taking his cue from Jack. "We've been out. Jack was enjoying being outside again."

"I hope you'll take good care out there," said Grandpa kindly. "Now, what was it you really wanted?"

Jack and Petros exchanged glances. Petros shrugged.

"We wanted to know what connects the Destiny Stone with the King's Cup," asked Jack simply.

"And what makes you think there's a connection?" demanded Doonya.

"Grandpa told me about an ancient cup in the Stone room. And the Icelandic elves told stories about it – and a magical globe."

"Come through to the living room," said Grandpa. "I think we all need to sit down."

"I'm not sure that you're ready to find out about this," began Doonya as they sat down in the front room, whereupon Grandpa Sandy held up his hand, a gesture that commanded immediate respect.

"Pierre."

Pierre. Uncle Doonya stiffened, recalling times when he'd been scolded as a young boy. His father only used his 'Sunday best' name when really serious – or angry.

"Young they may be, but stupid they are not," went on Grandpa. He faced the two youngsters. "The Stone is back, but things haven't improved as much as we expected. And since midsummer ancient manuscripts have appeared which confirm that the Stone is only one of three treasures." He looked intently at Jack. "Briannan was right after all. When the Stone is joined by the other two, a great power will be released. There's an ancient chalice or cup ..." He broke off. "I think we might as well let the rest of our audience in."

Without turning round, he flicked his right hand at the door, which promptly opened to reveal Rana and Lizzie crouching in the doorway. Both jumped up guiltily.

"Come in, girls," said their grandfather lightly. "I trust you've been enjoying the story?"

"We couldn't hear all of it," Lizzie began, only to be silenced by a sharp pinch from her sister.

"You may as well hear the rest in comfort. I take it that you are aware of the manuscripts?"

Rana nodded, while Lizzie looked away.

"They tell us that the Stone is linked to other treasures, including an ancient cup. I understand a symbol of this has been the prize in an annual match between Cos-Howe and Claville."

"The French captain sketched a fiery cup in the air before the game," said Jack. "Afterwards he went to claim it, but when his hands touched the flames, they disappeared. The referee disappeared too."

"Was there anything special about the cup?" asked Grandpa.

"Its markings," said Rana. "Afterwards I remembered where I'd seen them before – on Tamlina's ring."

Doonya and Katie turned sharply to look at Rana, their eyes wide with surprise.

"What do you know of Tamlina?" demanded Doonya angrily.

Sensing that she had strayed onto difficult ground, Rana hesitated.

"You'd better tell us what you know." Grandpa Sandy spoke gently.

"Ossian took us," explained Rana. "We didn't know where we were going, it was a secret. We just went along for some fun."

"I hope you realise how foolhardy that was," said Doonya. "Tamlina's a very dangerous enchantress. How did you know where she was?"

"Ossian knew," chimed in Lizzie. "She made Ossian and Petros wait behind while Rana and Jack and me went with her."

"She didn't give you anything to eat or drink, did she?" asked Aunt Katie anxiously.

"She gave us this broth, but we poured it out on the ground," said Jack. "She didn't notice; she'd already drunk hers."

"That's just as well, Jack dear. There's no knowing what might have happened if you'd drunk one of her potions."

"She went into a trance," continued Jack, "but it was hard to hear what she was saying."

"Something about a Trinity," broke in Rana. "And then she spoke of sphere and silver."

"She mentioned my father too," said Jack. "Something about him and Konan the Brashat trying to trick each other up in Keldy."

"I wish you'd told us this before, Jack," said his grandfather. "We haven't managed to get anything out of Tamlina before now. You must have caught her at a fortunate time."

"Afterwards, I don't think she remembered what she'd said," pointed out Lizzie. "She even asked us if she'd mentioned some kind of stone. She knew she'd been talking, because she said we had responsibility with knowledge."

"She was quite right, then," snapped her father. "The responsible thing would have been to come and tell us."

"So what does the Trinity mean then?" asked Petros. His parents looked at him, then at Grandpa Sandy.

"We're not sure." Grandpa tapped the fingertips of his left hand against those of his right. "The manuscripts are difficult to decipher, and there are many strange symbols. Rana," he turned to his granddaughter, "what were the markings on the King's Cup?"

"It was a round pattern," butted in Lizzie. "Three spirals joined in the middle."

"That's right," added Rana. "The same as Tamlina's ring. I'll draw it for you."

Rana fetched a pencil and a scrap of paper, and began to draw an outline of the shape.

As Rana presented her drawing, Grandpa and Uncle Doonya exchanged glances. Aunt Katie took the cue.

"Come on, you lot," she said, getting up. "We'll get you something to eat. Grandpa and Dad need a few moments to discuss things."

Reluctantly, the four youngsters went through to the kitchen. Each ate quickly but quietly, trying to listen for sounds from the front room. After ten minutes, Grandpa Sandy came through.

"You can come back in now," he announced. "Perhaps without realising it, you have uncovered important information. The Congress will have to decide what to do next."

"What do the spirals mean, Grandpa?" asked Petros, as they all sat down again.

"The manuscripts talk of a Trinity. The three spiral arms probably represent that. The Stone could be one arm, and the King's Cup another, but we're not sure if the third one is the globe. The documents are very old and difficult to read."

"Where did they come from?" asked Jack.

"That's a mystery," replied Doonya. "They appeared in the castle chapel a week after midsummer. Nobody knows how."

"Maybe a human left them," suggested Jack. "Humans walk through that chapel all day."

"That's possible," said Doonya. "Most of the manuscripts aren't Shian. That's why they're so hard to interpret."

"I can read human writing," piped up Rana.

"These aren't like the human books you've seen," said her mother kindly. "They're old parchments, from before the time printing was invented. That's what's so strange if it *was* a human who brought them. They must be valuable. Anybody could've picked them up."

"We must assume that whoever left them meant us to find them," said Grandpa. "The question is, why?"

"The Congress must decide," said Doonya. "There's only so much we can do on our own."

"I agree. But," said Grandpa, turning to the youngsters, "apart from telling the senior members of the Congress, this must be kept to ourselves. Having such knowledge could be dangerous if others know that we know. You must not tell anyone else what you have told us."

"We told Ossian what Tamlina had said," Jack pointed out.

"He hasn't told his parents, then," said Doonya. "Hart would certainly have let us know if he had. But has he told anyone else?"

"He's been on a tight rein since coming back from France," said Katie, "but I'm sure he'll still manage to meet his friends, and some of them are not that trustworthy."

"I'd better go to Keldy and find out," said Doonya. "I can go this evening."

"The Congress meets tonight," said Grandpa firmly. "You ought to be there."

"I'll be back in time for that. The Congress will want to know if anyone in Keldy knows all this."

Grandpa Sandy and Doonya returned late from the Congress meeting. Both looked drawn and tired. As they entered the house, Jack and Petros were getting ready to go upstairs.

"Just a moment, please, you two," said Doonya.

Exchanging puzzled glances, the two boys followed Doonya into the front room. Grandpa Sandy closed the door.

"How's Ossian?" asked Jack.

"He'll not be allowed out for a while," snapped Uncle Doonya. Then, composing himself, he continued, "Everyone in Keldy is fine. But things are happening that are causing us some concern."

"Tonight's Congress meeting was not plain sailing," explained Grandpa. "Our news has upset some people, and the upshot is that they want you both, and Rana and Lizzie, to appear before them next Friday."

Jack gulped hard. Apprentices were never summoned by the Congress, except for the most serious of offences.

"But why?" Petros found his voice first. "We haven't done anything wrong."

"It's not a matter of having done anything wrong," replied Grandpa, "although some believe that going to see Tamlina puts you in that category. But you have no choice. If summoned, you must attend. We'll be there too, so don't worry. I'm afraid," he continued, looking at Jack, "that in light of these events it would be safest for you not to leave the square until after next week's meeting."

"I've only just been allowed out!" shouted Jack. "That's not fair!" He thumped the arm of the sofa, and stormed out.

Both Jack and Petros found it hard to sleep that night. Indeed, the following week was difficult, with the Friday night meeting looming ahead. Rana alone seemed unconcerned, arguing that she hadn't committed any crime.

As Friday evening neared they were all made ready by Aunt Katie, to 'look their best' for the Congress. Jack, in his tidiest clothes, squirmed as his hair was once again brushed flat. He wasn't looking forward to being interviewed, but rationalised that the sooner they got there, the sooner it would be over.

Lizzie and Rana were arguing over whether they should take their pet squillo Nuxie along. Lizzie's claim that he was so sweet that he was bound to melt even the stoniest of Congress members' hearts was met with the withering retort that they didn't need luck. To Jack's relief, Grandpa Sandy arrived and announced that it was time to leave.

22
The Shian Congress

Grandpa Sandy assembled the group on the mound of earth at the foot of the square. Drawing his cloak around them, he whispered, "Wind-flock Cos-Howe."

Jack had no time to be surprised. The spinning and the loud drone started and finished so quickly that he had barely time to register where they were going. He was still feeling giddy as Grandpa Sandy lowered his cloak. The Cos-Howe entrance chamber was well lit this time, with a dozen burning torches on the wall.

"The meeting's here?" exclaimed Petros.

"The Congress meets as circumstances dictate," replied Grandpa, leading them towards the great wooden door. "I believe some senior Shian wish to impress on the Cos-Howe contingent that the Congress is in charge."

Jack saw that the tables that had been there on their previous visit had disappeared. Instead, one long wooden table at the far end faced them. Behind this were twelve high-backed wooden chairs, at which sat the Shian Congress.

They've all got the same cloak as Grandpa.

Starting at the left end, Jack saw Murkle and Rowan, conversing earnestly. Next to them sat a similarly old woman, whose wispy grey hair sprouted from underneath a small felt hat; then two gnomes, feverishly whispering with one other. Then an empty chair and an imposing throne, then two more empty chairs. Then a tall black woman with grey hair and a piercing gaze, who sat tapping her fingers rapidly on the table; then a Darrig who glowered as the group entered. Next to him, a hunched old man sat silently, his face hidden by his cloak hood. Jack tried to assess how friendly or hostile each would be.

The tall black woman stood up and indicated silently to Grandpa Sandy to join the table. As he moved to take an empty seat, he patted each youngster reassuringly on the shoulder.

Atholmor and Samara entered from a side door. Atholmor's cloak was a slightly brighter shade of green, but he wore the same dark tri-cornered hat as Grandpa. Everyone stood in silence until Atholmor had taken the throne, and Samara the seat between Grandpa and Armina, leaving vacant the seat to Atholmor's right.

Doonya went to the side of the great chamber, while Aunt Katie remained with the youngsters, facing the table.

"Don't worry," she whispered. "Just answer the questions, and we'll soon be out of here."

Jack noted that Cosmo was standing near Doonya, but that they were pointedly ignoring each other. Cosmo nodded silently at Jack, which made him feel a little better.

Atholmor tapped the table.

"This special meeting of the Congress is convened to hear from these young people."

"They have been meddling in things that should not concern them." Murkle rose from his chair. "In my day an apprentice would have been cast into iron for consorting with an enchantress."

"What do you mean, 'consorting'?" shouted the tall black woman.

"Please, Armina, Murkle, let us have order!" said Atholmor firmly. "These young people are not on trial. We merely wish to discover what they know." He faced the small group. "We understand that you were taken to see Tamlina, and that she drank some potion. We wish to know what she said while in a trance."

Jack moved confidently forward. "Tamlina only let me and Rana and Lizzie go with her. She drank her broth and went into a daze. She was mumbling something about my father and a Brashat trying to trick each other. Then she chanted about 'sphere and silver', and 'the Seat of Power'. That was it."

He stepped back to join the others.

The figure at the far right now removed the hood from his head. Jack looked up, and shuddered as he recognised the man who had looked in at Daid's window. The man's face had a long scar from below his right ear to the corner of his mouth, giving his face a sinister lopsided look.

"These children are mixing in dangerous company. Soon we'll have Brashat swarming all over because of them. They must be kept where they cannot put us all at risk – under lock and key, or else banished."

"Please, Finbogie, I have asked for good sense to prevail. I am aware that the Brashat have an interest in these matters, and like you I am keen not to let them too close to our secrets."

"What secrets?" snorted Murkle. "With these children meddling, nothing will remain secret for long."

"There is no doubt that these youngsters are well intentioned." Rowan's gentle voice was a heartening change from Murkle's. "I am sure that we would like to know what they have learned."

Jack relaxed. At least some of the Congress was on their side.

"What exactly did Tamlina say about 'sphere and silver'?" Atholmor spoke firmly.

Jack looked back at Rana and Lizzie. "If ... if sphere and silver they would gain ..." He paused, unable to recollect the rest.

"The Seat of Power they would win," concluded Rana promptly.

"Attain," Lizzie corrected her. "It's 'they would attain', not 'they would win'."

"Same difference," said Rana huffily.

"Thank you, young ladies," said Atholmor. "Now, she mentioned a Brashat by name, is that right?"

"That's right. Konan," replied Jack. "She said him and my father were travelling through Keldy trying to trick each other."

"Tamlina will have killed them both," said Finbogie with what might have been a satisfied look. "She's not to be trusted."

"Thank you, Finbogie," said Atholmor evenly. "That does not help us." Turning back to the youngsters, he continued, "Now I also understand that you saw a ring on Tamlina's hand. Could you describe it?"

Aunt Katie stepped forward and placed Rana's sketch of the pattern on the table. Atholmor inspected this, then passed it along towards Murkle, who sat silently at the end.

"Murkle, I don't recognise this symbol, and yet it is clearly important, or Tamlina would not have worn such a ring."

As the Shian history expert, Murkle was evidently the one to consult. His frown changed to a look of expectation. As the piece of paper reached him, he grasped it eagerly, but the anticipation on his face died almost immediately. Eventually, and with a heavy heart, he admitted, "I do not know this symbol. I do not believe it to be Shian."

A buzz ran along the length of the table. Atholmor leant towards Grandpa Sandy and whispered in his ear. Grandpa continued to stare ahead of him, and nodded slowly. Jack looked across at Aunt Katie, who shrugged her shoulders. After a moment, Atholmor spoke again.

"We need to consider this. If the symbol is not Shian, we must find out its significance."

"What do they know about the King's Cup?" demanded Finbogie.

"It's a piece of Dameve trickery," said the old woman with the shawl. "The Cup was stolen from us, and the fools have lost it."

"Thank you, Ban-Eye, please do not insult our human neighbours in that way, particularly with the young people here." Atholmor once again spoke firmly, emphasising his authority. He looked at Petros. "Now, you went to France where you saw the Cup, is that right?"

"It was just a fiery outline," said Petros. "It disappeared when the French captain tried to grab it. Everyone laughed then, like they knew it would happen."

Atholmor turned now to Cosmo, who had remained silently standing by the side wall. "Is that right? The cup is just an imitation?"

"There's no secret about it," said Cosmo, stepping forward. "We play for the fiery cup every year. The real Cup disappeared long ago – everyone knows that."

"But is there anything distinguishing about this replica?" asked Atholmor.

"It's just a goblet. It's got some funny symbols across the base of the bowl."

"Like Tamlina's ring," shouted Rana. "It's the same pattern! They're all the way round the bowl . . ." Her voice trailed off as she saw the look of astonishment on the faces of the Congress members.

"What?!" shouted the old woman with the shawl. "That's a lie. The Cup is Shian, and those Dameves have added something to it. Just let them come to my woods – I'll show them what terror is."

"Ban-Eye, I have asked that that language is *not* used here," said Atholmor wearily. "We are the Congress, the Seelie Court, and we have certain standards to maintain."

"And where have your standards got us, Atholmor?" challenged Finbogie. "The Brashat disrupt the Seventh, you tolerate them having one of their boys as an apprentice under the castle and we suspect they are after the Stone, and yet you do nothing about it. It's time we sent them packing."

"Finbogie, as you well know we have our reasons for allowing the Brashat boy to study under the castle," said Atholmor with a sigh.

"You would have a war with the Unseelie, is that it, Finbogie?" Murkle spoke in an even voice. "Do you need reminding of what happens when the Shian fight each other?"

"Atholmor, these discussions should not be in front of the children." Samara spoke for the first time, and there was a moment's silence along the table. Jack had been watching this debate develop with a mixture of fascination and misgiving. The Congress was the most important body of Shian in this part of the country, and here they were, arguing like ... well, like children.

Atholmor reflected for a moment then beckoned Doonya forward, who bent down so that Atholmor could whisper in his ear. Jack saw his grandfather nod at Doonya, who then turned and paced towards the youngsters.

"We'll wait outside a while," he announced, shepherding them back towards the large wooden door.

"Is Cosmo staying, then?" asked Petros.

"Cosmo's got some information about the Cup."

"He's said all he knows," said Rana dismissively as they left the great chamber, "and that wasn't much. Honestly, he didn't even know about the Cup's markings, and he's seen it loads of times."

"The Cup was just a symbol to him, he knew it wasn't real," pointed out Jack. "So what do those spiral shapes mean anyway, if you're so clever?"

"I don't know," retorted Rana, "but they're important, aren't they, Dad?"

"Yes, they are," replied Doonya. "Now, we'll just wait here until we're called back."

"Does the Congress always argue like that?" said Jack.

"You've caught the Congress at a difficult time," answered Doonya evasively. "It's like Grandpa said: things are changing, and not everyone likes that."

"Grandpa said the Cup tells secrets of life and death. And anyway, humans don't think death is the end. They go on living somewhere else afterwards," said Jack.

Jack gasped for breath as Rana, looking daggers at him, dug him sharply with her elbow, and he realised that his aunt was wiping tears from her eyes. Doonya had put his arm around Katie's shoulders, and Lizzie was hugging her waist. Jack looked at Petros, who shrugged, as if to say, "What did I tell you?"

"Not all the humans believe that," said his uncle. "Even for those who do, death can be frightening."

"How come Fenrig's allowed under the castle?" Jack tried to change the subject.

Doonya pulled at his earlobe. While aware that Atholmor had alluded to certain reasons for Fenrig's presence, he evidently didn't want to give more away. His unease was helped by Grandpa Sandy opening the wooden door and beckoning them all back in.

As they took their places facing the table, Atholmor spoke. "My young friends, I am sorry that you have not seen us in better circumstances. We have to steer a course in troubled waters. Cosmo here has explained the story of the fiery cup, but he is unable to tell us what patterns were on this symbol."

"We didn't get a good look at the cup. It disappeared when the French captain tried to grab it," said Jack.

"Tamlina mentioned devils from Adam's race too," said Rana. "And someone else, 'the Grey', she said."

"The Grey!" shrieked Finbogie dramatically. "That's all we need. She'll have joined forces with the Brashat. We must take action."

There was renewed muttering and chatter along the length of the table.

"If there's work to be done with the Grey," said Armina, her eyes sparkling fiercely, "then I will do it."

"Thank you, Armina," said Atholmor firmly. "But first, let us conclude with these young people. Can you tell us anything else about what Tamlina said?"

"When she woke up, she mentioned a stone. Rag-something."

There was a pause while the Congress members looked blankly at each other. Finally, Atholmor spoke.

"It'll have been one of her charm stones; she must have hundreds. Was there nothing else?"

The four youngsters looked at each other, then, feeling that they had nothing new to add, Jack said, "No, sir."

"Thank you for coming along tonight. You have brought us important information. Now maybe your uncle and aunt can take you home. Thank you, Cosmo, you may also go now."

23
Matters of Life and Theft

Back at the house, everyone flopped down into the chairs in the front room. Only Rana had not been overawed by the evening's events.

"We'd done nothing wrong," she reasoned. "And they said we helped."

"Finbogie was horrible," said Rana. "Why do old people get like that?"

"He can be quite fierce," said Doonya. "You saw his scar? He got that battling a Dunter, long ago."

"He said we should be banished," said Petros heatedly. "That's not fierce, that's mean. I'll get him one day."

"That's enough, Petros!" snapped Doonya. "We're all on the same side."

Petros muttered under his breath.

"What about Armina?" said Lizzie. "She said she'd take on 'the Grey'. That's brave, isn't it?"

"Who's 'the Grey'?" asked Jack. "I never understood that bit."

"The Grey's been around for centuries," said Katie. "She's like an enchantress, only more powerful. And dangerous. A lot of people – Shian and human – end up dead if they get too close to her."

"I'm sorry for talking about humans dying," said Jack. "I'd forgotten it upsets you."

"That's all right, Jack dear. I think we'd better explain a few things to you. Let me get some juice and biscuits for you all."

Once they had their refreshments, Katie began.

"You all know that humans don't live as long as Shian. And my father wasn't very old when he died. Petros, I know Daid teaches you about this: what's one of the big differences between Shian and humans?"

Petros thought for a moment. "You mean, how they think about death? Well, Shian can live for hundreds of years, but when they die no one knows what happens. Dad's told me about the island, where some people think they go."

"That's right. Nanog," said Katie. "We don't know if it's true, because if Shian do go there, they never come back. Some, like the Brashat, don't believe in that at all. They believe that when we die, that's it, nothing."

"So nobody really knows?" said Rana incredulously. "Why's everybody so upset, then?"

"Because of all this talk of the Cup, and its power over life and death," said her father patiently. "That's a prize Shian will fight for, but the Stone has not brought us the strength we thought it would."

"You heard Tamlina talking of a sphere too, isn't that right?" said Katie.

"What's that got to do with dying?"

"The manuscripts tell of a great power when three treasures come together," said Katie. "We have the Stone; the fiery cup has reawakened interest in the real Cup, because whoever has that might be able to control death. If you add in the Sphere showing your true path – that's a powerful combination."

The silence was broken by Grandpa appearing at the door of the front room.

"All here? I thought the young ones might have gone to bed."

"We were just discussing the three treasures," said Doonya. "They need to know what we're up against."

"You have certainly helped the Congress tonight." Grandpa Sandy looked at the four youngsters keenly. "We must find the Cup, and the Sphere if we can, and bring them here, where they'll be safe."

"Safe from who?" demanded Petros.

"From those Unseelie who would wish to control life and death. For us, and the humans," replied Grandpa evenly.

"So what do we do now?" asked Jack.

"You continue your studies. Perhaps you can discover the whereabouts of these treasures."

"We're just apprentices," said Petros plaintively. "Shouldn't the Congress be doing that?"

"He's right," said Katie to Doonya. "They're too young to be taking this on. They should leave things to the Congress."

"Although a strong Congress is needed to keep the Unseelie parts of the country in check, as you saw, the Congress is not as united as it should be," said Grandpa.

"Then what chance have *we* got?" demanded Petros.

"You have lessons with Daid, don't you? The secret may be there. Or indeed with Murkle and his tales."

Jack groaned at this. "What have the manuscripts told us so far about the Cup?" he asked. "The replica's no use."

"The manuscripts talk of a human journey with the Cup." Doonya stood up. "A journey to a cave, and death followed it. If we can find the cave, we may get somewhere."

Over the weekend Grandpa, Doonya, Jack and Petros sat huddled in the front room, discussing where the cave might be, but without inspiration or success. Rana and Lizzie protested that it was unfair to exclude them, and their mother's attempts to entice them out for a shopping expedition along the High Street were met with scorn. Mealtimes were sullen affairs.

As Jack and Petros set off for their workshops on Monday morning, Rana's voice called after them. "Don't you worry about us, we'll be fine, stuck here with nothing to do all day. You go off and enjoy yourselves."

Petros gave Jack a resigned look, and turned into Cormac's house. As Jack neared Gilmore's workshop, he saw the tailor standing by the door.

"Come in," he said, but without his usual good humour.

Jack looked quizzically at Freya, who just shrugged. Fenrig and Doxer stood beside her, both looking down at their feet.

"I am very sorry to report that some cloth has been stolen." Gilmore avoided looking at any one of the four youngsters. "In all my years of teaching apprentices I have only once had to deal with theft before. This is not something we expect of apprentices here."

Nonplussed, Jack looked at his colleagues. Freya didn't look worried, but fidgeted with a square of silk. Doxer was silent, and continued to stare at the table. Only Fenrig dared reply.

"How d'you know? There's piles of stuff all over this place."

"The 'stuff', as you call it, is expensive, some of it rare." Gilmore fixed him with his eye. "I have been teaching you how to look after it, to know it and care for it. It would appear that you do not have the qualities to make a good tailor. Now, have you removed any cloths from this workshop?"

Fenrig stared back. "I don't need your stupid cloths. So what are you going to do about it?"

"I will contact your father and ask him to remove you. It is clear you do not wish to learn this trade."

"My father's not going to be pleased if you send me away. Not pleased at all," sneered Fenrig.

Gilmore paused, evidently weighing this up. Eventually he spoke again. "I will see you first thing tomorrow morning. I suggest you find something else to do until Murkle's lesson."

Fenrig sloped off, and the others took their places at the table. Finally, after a strained silence, Gilmore spoke again. "I will not tolerate theft. Is that understood?"

Jack and Freya mumbled assent, and set to work on their cloths.

When Gilmore had gone to his house for lunch, Jack and Freya discussed Fenrig's dismissal.

"Gilmore will never expel him," said Freya matter-of-factly. "My dad told me Fenrig's father and Gilmore go back a long way. Briannan's supposed to be smart, but Fenrig's an idiot. He was bound to get caught sooner or later."

"You know he was stealing?"

"I've seen him slipping bits of cloth into his satchel. I'm surprised Gilmore didn't notice before."

"Why didn't you say something?"

"None of my business," said Freya casually. "Besides, it's useful having someone as stupid as him here. Helps distract Gilmore." She looked at Jack evenly.

Jack examined her face, but couldn't work out what she had meant by this.

Murkle's lesson that afternoon lived down to expectations. After an hour and a half of sheer boredom, Murkle dismissed the class, but asked Jack to stay behind. As the last youngster left, Murkle went back to his chair.

"I trust you are not going to be over-ambitious in the matter we discussed?" he asked brusquely.

"Wha—what d'you mean?" Jack tried to look evenly at his tutor, but his voice betrayed him.

"I mean there are things that are the concern of the Congress, not of young apprentices, and you have already meddled with very dangerous people. You may be brave, but do not be stupid."

"I just want to find my father," said Jack, turning to the door.

"Jack." The unexpectedly friendly tone halted Jack in his tracks. "Be careful."

Jack turned and looked at Murkle, but there was nothing in the tutor's demeanour to suggest that he had even spoken.

When Jack got home, he reported the story to his grand-father, who shrugged.

"I never could make Murkle out. He's clever enough, but completely without charm. But if push came to shove, I'm sure he'd be on the right side."

"Gilmore thinks Fenrig's been stealing," said Jack. "He's threatened to expel him."

"As you know, the Congress has its reasons for allowing Fenrig to be here. For a start, it allows the Brashat to think they've achieved something. And you can keep an eye on him."

"He disappears after class. I don't know where he goes."

"Nevertheless, keep a close watch on him. I've heard he speaks carelessly; you might learn a great deal."

Jack pondered this. "When are we going travelling, Grandpa? You said we could go and find out things."

"Equinox is at the end of next week. The time will be right then. In the meantime, see if Daid can throw any light on the Cup. Remember it's called the King's Chalice in some stories."

However, Jack was to get no chance to ask Daid any questions, for his teacher was mysteriously absent on the Thursday when the apprentices met outside his house.

"How're you getting on with your book?" asked Purdy as she and Jack walked slowly back down the square.

"It's too long, I should've chosen something shorter. Bits are interesting, but it just goes on and on."

"Mine's not bad. This rich lady kept a diary when she went travelling around the north lands. She even talks about some of the humans who mixed with the Shian. I think that's why Daid has the book."

Jack's ears pricked up. "I didn't know the humans were that interested in us."

"Not many are. You can borrow the book if you like. I've nearly finished it."

"No thanks," said Jack. "I've got enough to read with my book."

The next few days passed slowly. Fenrig continued to appear at Gilmore's, but nothing more was said about his presence or the stolen cloths. Jack couldn't concentrate. He was itching to get away again, to feel the fresh air on his face. It made him feel free. Being cooped up wasn't helping his mood, and he snapped frequently. Rana and Lizzie's attempt at a simple levitation hex was met with a withering retort, and Aunt Katie's encouragement to finish his meals only brought on grumpiness.

After what felt like the longest week of his life, the day of the autumn equinox and the trip to Keldy finally arrived. Jack's heart raced at the thought of the 'little walk in the woods' Grandpa had planned for the boys.

Doonya led Katie and the girls to the low road mound. Jack watched as his uncle's cloak enveloped the small group, and then witnessed the spinning that seemed to start from under the cloak before all four disappeared.

"Us next," said Grandpa, and the three of them stepped onto the mound.

"Wind-flock Keldy."

The others were waiting for them. Rana, grinning widely, had clearly enjoyed the journey. Lizzie looked peaky, but seemed determined not to give this away.

"Come on, they'll be waiting for us at the house," said Katie.

The group of seven made their way along the path, and soon found themselves in the big house.

"Oh, it's good to see you," beamed Aunt Dorcas. "It seems like ages since you were here."

"Only three months," said Rana. "Just after midsummer. Can you show Lizzie and me how you do your baking?"

Petros looked questioningly at Jack. His sisters were not usually so keen on domestic affairs.

"Are you two feeling all right?" he asked, only half-jokingly.

"Oh yes," said Rana nonchalantly "I'm sure you've got things to do. We'll just get on with some home cooking. We can have things ready for when you get back."

This sounded suspiciously keen to Petros and Jack, but Aunt Katie was delighted. "Oh good," she said. "We can do all sorts while the men are away."

"We'd better be going," said Hart.

The others followed him, and within minutes were heading into the woods.

"Are you sure you know where she is?" asked Doonya.

"A grig told me two days ago," replied Ossian. "She collects roots at equinox by the big hawthorn. I told the grig to pass word that you'd be comin'."

"How many did you say there would be?" enquired Grandpa.

"I didn't say a number, just that Jack from Rangie and some family would be there."

"What?! You mentioned Jack by name?" demanded Doonya.

"She's met him before. I thought that made sense," replied Ossian huffily.

"The last time she met him she tried to give him some kind of potion," pointed out Grandpa. "And it wasn't hawberry juice."

They walked on in silence. Suddenly a buzzing noise was heard, and a grig flew in and made towards Hart. The tiny creature perched on his shoulder, and a whispered conversation took place.

"What is it?" asked Grandpa as the grig flew off.

"It's Dorcas. Something's happened at the house. I'd better go back." Hart turned to Ossian. "You take care, you hear? Don't be taking unnecessary risks."

24
Equinox

After several minutes they came to the clearing where they had waited on their previous visit.

"She'll send a grig when she's ready," announced Ossian. He sat down and began pulling pieces of twine into snares.

Jack leant against a tree stump and started to peel bark off the dead wood. Petros, quickly bored, began stamping on dead branches. Sitting around in the woods was not his idea of fun, and he mused longingly on Edinburgh's many attractions.

They had waited about twenty minutes when Jack thought he heard a rustling and a low giggle behind him. He turned round, but saw nothing unusual. Ossian stood up and stretched. He began whistling, tunelessly. After a couple of minutes of this low monotonous sound, Doonya snapped, "Can't you be quiet?!"

"I'm callin' someone," Ossian shrugged, and resumed his whistling. Within seconds, a small antelope-like creature had emerged from the trees, making a soft purring noise.

Jack looked at the animal. Like a roe deer in shape, it had a strange mixture of colours – brown, red, grey, yellow – and a small horn between its eyes. He whispered to Petros, "What is it? It's too small for a unicorn."

"*Tappa, Kirin*," said Ossian soothingly. He turned to the others. "This is the Kirin. He's come to say the History Pool waters are disturbed."

Grandpa turned with interest. "Indeed. I have myself only once seen them in that state. How far off are they?"

"About a mile. I've never seen them like this before. Who wants to come?"

"We have to see Tamlina," said Doonya urgently. "Who knows when we'll get another chance?"

Grandpa Sandy, evidently torn between two impulses, reflected for a moment, then said, "Pierre, you go with Ossian and watch the waters. They may have something to tell us."

"All right. But if there's not much happening when we get there, I'm coming back."

Once Ossian and Doonya had followed the Kirin into the woods, Jack turned to his grandfather.

"Grandpa, where'd that creature come from? I've never seen one before."

"The Kirin come from Japan. They're said to bring judgement – punishment and reward. I've never seen one before, either. Young Ossian certainly has a way with creatures."

"What's the History Pool?" asked Petros.

"It's a pool which reveals stories from the past. When the circumstances are right, the waters get ruffled; when they clear, they reveal pictures of mysteries. There's no knowing what it may tell, but it's certainly worth investigating."

"Is it like that time your simul–simul-something . . ."

"Simulacrum?"

Jack nodded. In his mind's eye he could see again the tableau of silent figures as they played out the history of the Stone.

"No, Jack. Those pictures showed what I could remember. But sometimes what you think is true isn't true at all. My memories created those pictures, and memories can distort. The History Pool only ever shows the truth. Now, I wish that enchantress would let us speak to her."

After what seemed like ages, a flurry of tiny wings heralded another grig. It flew up to Grandpa and perched on his shoulder. He took out a tiny biscuit from his pocket and gave it to the creature.

"We can proceed," he said quietly to the two boys. "But carefully, all right? I am not altogether certain that we can trust Tamlina. We are to follow the path to the west."

The barely visible path was not the one the boys had used in their earlier encounter. They walked on in silence for several minutes, when an abrupt voice commanded them, "Halt!"

Obediently, they all stopped. After a pause, the voice resumed.

"Did ye think ye could trick me, Sandy o' the Stone? I will not be made a fool of."

Grandpa Sandy looked perplexed. "Tamlina," he said, "we mean no harm, and we have attempted no trickery."

Tamlina's form appeared in front of them. She looked as she had the first time Jack had seen her: black-cloaked, her dirty hair fell down over her face and shoulders.

"I sense five o' ye," she said slowly. "Where are the ithers?"

"They went to investigate the History Pool," explained Grandpa. "The Kirin told our companions that the waters were disturbed."

Tamlina's eyes narrowed. "Very well," she said warily, "whit is't ye wish tae know?"

Jack was relieved to see that there was no potion brewing nearby. He saw too that Tamlina wore the Triple-S ring on her finger. Nudging Petros, he indicated her hand with his head.

"You know well that we have been the Watchers of the Stone for many years. Manuscripts have been found that talk of the Stone and other treasures. We wish to know about the King's Chalice, and of a magical sphere. Also," and at this Grandpa looked cautiously at Jack and Petros, "we wish to find out about Gosol."

Petros looked up. That was the name he had heard his father and grandfather mention back under the castle. Tamlina appeared to consider this request for a while.

"There's little mystery aboot the King's Chalice," she said eventually. "The answer's under the castle. Did ye not realise that these matters concern the humans too? Ye should seek yer expert on human concerns."

Then, in a slow chanting voice, she intoned, "As the moon shall rise on the Eve of All Hallows, so is revealed the great King's Chalice."

Her eyes had glazed over for a brief moment while she chanted, but this quickly passed, and she resumed speaking. "The Sphere will be revealed in the fullness o' time. And Gosol is the key tae all three treasures. Oor destiny is mixed up wi' all o' creation."

"You mean the humans?" demanded Petros.

"Foolish child!" A bolt emerged from Tamlina's right hand, and Petros fell, stunned.

Jack shrank back instinctively as Grandpa Sandy drew his sceptre and prepared to return fire, but Tamlina fell back herself with an audible gasp. She sat on the ground for a moment, wheezing softly. Getting awkwardly to her feet, she moved forward and helped Petros up again. Grandpa lowered his sceptre, watching her carefully.

"Ye made me lose my temper, young man," she said in a calm voice. "In times past ye might niver have walked again. But times are changin', and some o' the old ways are goin'. Dae ye forgive me?"

Jack and his grandfather were almost as stunned as Petros had been. For an enchantress to carry out a punishment and then ask for forgiveness was unheard of. Petros's mouth opened and shut, but no words came out. Grandpa Sandy rescued the situation.

"Tamlina, this is most charitable. Petros should have held his tongue. To ask his forgiveness astonishes us. Might I ask why this change has come about?"

Tamlina looked at him intently. "Sandy o' the Stone, I think ye ken the answer tae that. The manuscripts ye hae seen talk o' Gosol, do they not?" Grandpa Sandy inclined his head. "And ye ken that Gosol binds together all o' creation."

The quizzical looks of Grandpa and the others prompted her to continue.

"In the heavens, and on the earth, and under the earth, all o' creation meets. My Raglan telt me that. And Shian and human can mix. But be warned: it's a blessin', and a curse."

"That doesn't make sense," blurted Jack.

"But Gosol resolves all such. Look again at all the papers under the castle. If ye seek, ye will fin' the Cup; that may lead ye tae the Sphere. In the fullness o' time ye may discern creation's mystery."

Seeing that Jack was clearly bursting to speak, Grandpa looked hard at him and shook his head slowly, but Jack stepped forward and raised his hand. His blue eye burned fiercely, and he looked Tamlina directly in the face. She stared back, her mouth half smiling.

"Yer eyes are distinctive, young man. I believe we have met before?"

"I–I have been here before," stammered Jack, "to find out about my father, Phineas of Rangie. But can I ask one question?"

Tamlina nodded assent.

"Your ring: what does it mean?"

Tamlina paused, and looked down at the large ring.

"Good things come in threes," she said, then paused. Then, in a sing-song voice she chanted:

> *A Frenchman's great cup was elsewhere besides,*
> *Its fortunes beset by warfare and tides,*
> *A king's chosen vessel, a thief's brief reward,*
> *Its future determined by fire and by sword.*

Tamlina paused again, then mumbled, "I tire. Soon ye may fin' the Cup. But be warned, for ithers seek it. Young Jack, perhaps ye ha'e already met Konan o' the Brashat? Saddux like him will fight ye. And ye will never fin' them forgivin'. Tak' ye this ram's horn. One night it may help ye tae summon allies in yer quest."

She handed Jack a polished ram's horn, with a small mouth-piece at one end.

"Tak' care. The winnin' o' the Chalice will demand brave hearts."

With that Tamlina faded from their eyes.

"That hurt," Petros grumbled, rubbing his chest.

"What was that about Konan the Brashat? I've never met him." Jack's mind raced. "And what kind of allies will a ram's horn bring? She was so different this time. I mean, I know she zapped Petros, but then she apologised. Why would she do that, Grandpa?"

"Times are changing," frowned Grandpa. "And we may not have much time to find out what we need. If the Brashat are after the Cup, then we must hurry."

He set off briskly back the way they had come.

"She talked of the Raglan again, Grandpa," said Jack, panting slightly as he tried to keep up.

"It'll be a charm stone – we told you before."

"What did she mean, 'the Saddux'?" asked Petros, following on.

"It is an old word signifying those who believe that death is the end," replied Grandpa. "It refers to Shian and humans. It seems we are more bound up than ever before."

"Aunt Katie said the Brashat think death is the end," said Jack. "So I guess they want the Cup because they think that means they'll never die."

"Grandpa, can't we slow down a bit?" said Petros. "I'm out of breath."

"Then perhaps it would be best to save your questions for later. I need time to think about what Tamlina has told us.

Look after that horn she gave you, Jack. Tamlina will always have a reason for doing things."

As they reached the house they saw people standing at the doorway, talking and laughing; the sound of music came from inside. As they entered, they found the house packed. Hart and Dorcas were in the kitchen, singing together while a young fiddler played along. People were listening with rapt attention. The atmosphere resonated with goodwill.

"What was the problem?" asked Grandpa of Hart when his song finished.

Hart looked blank for a moment. "Oh, that. Those two," he indicated Rana and Lizzie in the doorway, "were playing truant. As soon as we'd left, they just disappeared. Dorcas was worried sick."

Jack looked across to where his cousins were scoffing cakes. Rana saw him looking and waved, laughing.

"And where were they?" asked Jack.

"They won't say, except it was 'in the woods playing'. They had Dorcas and Katie going for a while. But no harm done."

"There are things we should discuss," said Grandpa to Hart. "Where are Ossian and Doonya?"

"They sent a grig to say they'd be late. But it's the party now. We can talk in the morning."

Jack and Petros made a beeline for the food. It had been a good day: they had been to see an enchantress, apart from the zap (secretly Petros was quite proud of this) she had treated them well, times were changing and they felt part of it, important.

When the sun had gone down and twilight was just upon them, people started to move outside for the moment when day and night would meet on equal terms. In the western sky, a meteor shower heralded the moment when the year turned into a new quarter. All raised their goblets to the sky and chorused, "Equinox!"

25
A Mystery Explained

Jack half-awoke at dawn and could hear his grandfather and uncles talking downstairs, but he was too tired to get up. When he came down for breakfast two hours later and pressed them for information, Doonya seemed irritable.

"Not now, Jack. We've got to get back to the castle. We must consult the manuscripts, and you'll be late if we don't get a move on."

"He's right," Grandpa concurred.

Jack ate in silence. They had all shared in yesterday's adventure, surely they should all discuss what they knew? But the adults were not for changing their minds, and after a hurried breakfast, they set out for the low road. Striding ahead, Doonya got to the mound first.

"Come on," he announced sharply. "You have your apprenticeships to go to, and we have much to do."

As Rana and Lizzie caught up, taking as long as they dared,

Grandpa ushered them towards their parents on the low road entrance.

"Come along, girls," he said quickly. "You need to get going too."

Doonya put his arms around their shoulders.

"Wind-flock castle!"

Within seconds, Jack and Petros were also flying back to the castle with Grandpa. By the time they reached the Shian square, Rana and Lizzie had run ahead to the house, eager to check that Nuxie was all right. Jack and Petros had time only to pick up their satchels and make off for their morning's work.

When Jack reached Gilmore's workshop, the only other person there was Freya.

"Hiya, Jack," she called. "Did you have a good time at Keldy last night? We heard your aunt and uncle were having a party."

"It was great. We went into the woods again to see ..." Jack's voice trailed off. Should he be telling others what they had done?

"It's all right, you don't have to say." Freya saved him the embarrassment of trying to back down. "I'll hear anyway; your cousins can't keep a secret."

"If you mean Rana and Lizzie, they didn't come with us," said Jack curtly, and was surprised when Freya just smiled back.

"Gilmore's not going to be in 'til later, and Doxer's sick today. D'you want to see some special cloth?"

Jack looked around. It was certainly quieter than usual.

"Where's Fenrig?"

"Dunno. He suits himself most of the time. I don't think he's been sent home, though. Come here. I'll show you what I'm working on."

Jack examined the dark green shiny bonnet Freya was sewing. The cloth almost glowed.

"It's a shifter," explained Freya. "When you put it on, you move sideways or backwards ten or fifteen yards. It's for getting you out of a tight spot. You have to be quick, though, and keep moving. Whoever's after you won't wait around."

"Can I try it?"

"It's not finished yet. I might let you try it in a few days. But don't say anything to Gilmore. You know how strict he is."

Gilmore, when he finally arrived, was flustered, and not inclined to speak. When Jack asked what he should do next, Gilmore snapped back irritably that Jack was old enough to find things to do for himself.

Jack's day was not improved by Murkle's lesson. Once again the great storyteller launched into a lengthy tale about a brave Shian prince, and once again his room became a sleepy retreat from the outside world for several young apprentices. Most had stopped listening after a few minutes and were trying to find something – anything – to hold their attention. Jack sat and thought about Tamlina's chant.

"*A thief's brief reward.*" So someone had stolen the Cup. Well, that didn't help much. Who? And where was it now? "*Its future determined by fire and by sword.*" Jack resolved to ask Grandpa about this as soon as the lesson ended. And what about the ram's horn? If it was that important, he would have to keep it with him at all times. He must have been thinking hard about the visit to Keldy, because mercifully the time slipped by quickly. However, when he got home, his aunt informed him that Grandpa was not likely to be back until much later.

"He's got things to see to, dear," she explained. "And I'm not sure you young ones should be getting mixed up in all this."

Rana and Lizzie were playing noisily in the front room. Jack went in to see what they were up to.

"We know something you don't," teased Lizzie.

"Heard it," said Jack, refusing to rise to the bait.

"Did you enjoy your trip to see you-know-who yesterday?" asked Rana innocently.

"What d'you mean? Who're you talking about?"

"Oh, nothing," replied Rana airily. "We just thought maybe you wanted to tell us some of your stories." She eyed him playfully. "She did keep you waiting an awful long time, though."

"It *was* you, wasn't it?" shouted Jack. "One time I was sure I'd heard you. How'd you manage it?"

"Manage what?" said Lizzie, her eyes wide open in fake surprise.

"You know what I mean," said Jack, recovering his poise. "You followed us, didn't you? And Tamlina nearly discovered you too. She sensed five of us there."

"You mean you went to see that old hag?" asked Rana in a mock serious voice, but, unable to keep a straight face, she promptly burst out laughing, and was joined by her sister.

Realising he would get nowhere with them on his own, Jack resolved to wait for Petros. But his cousin was late that day, only turning up when Uncle Doonya and Grandpa returned at suppertime. As they all sat around the table, Rana and Lizzie kept giggling and whispering to each other. Catching the flow of Jack's increasing exasperation, Grandpa forestalled any shouting.

"Jack, we'll have a chat after supper about yesterday. I'm sorry, but there really wasn't time this morning."

After supper, Grandpa ushered Jack, Petros and Doonya into the front room.

"Jack," he began, stroking his beard, "we have some news for you. Your uncle and Ossian went to the History Pool, as you know. And Doonya has something to tell you."

"Word had got around, and there were many creatures by the Pool. But it knows who's watching, somehow. When it was our turn we looked in, and ..." He took a deep breath. "We saw your father, Jack. Going through the woods of Keldy all those years ago with Konan the Brashat. And it's like Tamlina told you. They were trying to trick each other."

Jack's felt his heart jump up his throat. For years he had wanted to find out about his father; now he dreaded hearing more.

"Your father and Konan started arguing, then fighting, then the Grey arrived."

Jack gasped.

"She quickly suspended the two of them. We saw them hanging, frozen, in the dark. Then the waters became murky again. When they cleared, it was just your father there."

"Jack," Grandpa's voice was soothing. "It tells us he didn't betray us. And although the Grey's curse is strong, there may be ways to break it."

"What ... what did he look like?" Jack knew it was an odd question, but his brain was having trouble processing this new information.

"Jack, he was suspended," said Doonya softly. "It's like the body is frozen – it looks lifeless."

"But you get suspended for committing serious crimes."

"It's the Grey we're dealing with, Jack. She makes her own rules."

"What can break the curse?" whispered Jack.

"Until we find him, that's impossible to say," said Grandpa gently. "It depends what the Grey has done to him. He looked suspended. There may be more. But her power is not absolute, she *can* be beaten."

"How did Konan escape, then?" asked Petros. "Maybe the Brashat did a deal with the Grey."

"The Grey doesn't 'do' deals. She's an agent of despair and death," said Doonya. "Being a Brashat won't protect you from that."

"But the Brashat do live longer than us, don't they?" pointed out Petros. "That might mean they have some influence with death."

"They *want* influence with death – that's why I'm sure they'd like to get the Cup. They'll think it'll let them live forever. But they don't have it yet. And the Grey cursed both of them. We don't know how Konan got away."

"Tamlina said I might have met Konan," said Jack softly. "But I would know if I had, wouldn't I?"

"Tamlina speaks in riddles sometimes – who knows what she meant? There are many things we still have to figure out, including where the Cup is. She was specific about asking Daid's advice, though. He was away for Equinox, but he'll be back tomorrow."

Jack's head was buzzing as he made his way upstairs for bed. He didn't feel like talking about it, not even to Petros. Rana and Lizzie were playing up in the next bedroom, until Katie shouted at them to be quiet. Jack was grateful for the comparative quiet as he lay there, trying to make sense of his thoughts. But no matter how he tried, he couldn't work out what he was meant to be feeling.

Jack had a restless night. A series of bizarre dreams prevented any restful sleep, and when morning came he felt bleary. His work at Gilmore's did not go well, his basic mistakes exasperating his tutor. By the time Jack got home that afternoon he felt drained, and even passed up the chance to go out to the High Street, slumping instead in the front room, alone. His mood didn't improve at suppertime when Grandpa announced that Daid had not provided any useful information.

"I couldn't tell you over supper," explained Grandpa to the boys afterwards. "The girls are a little young to be hearing this, but as you are both already taught by Daid, I feel it's fair to tell you."

Jack and Petros exchanged puzzled glances.

"You may have noticed that Daid is not always ... alert," stated Grandpa. Jack smiled quietly. "He has an unparalleled experience of living with humans, but that experience has left him with an occasional disadvantage. He has a fondness, shall we say, for some of the human failings."

"You mean he likes their beer?" laughed Petros. "Everyone in my class knows that."

"Your classmates may have noticed something," continued Grandpa evenly, "but you ought to know that Shian can't drink human beer."

Jack saw his cousin blush.

"That said, Daid has developed something of a taste for what the humans call the water of life – a spirit drink. The upshot is that sometimes – like now – he's a little under the weather. We won't get much out of him until tomorrow. However, we still have time. Tamlina said the Cup is revealed on Hallows' Eve, that's not for another month."

Grandpa's optimism, however, was unfounded, for even the next day Daid was unable to provide any useful information. By the time Thursday's lesson came around, Daid was almost beside himself with worry. He spent the entire lesson jumping up and rushing over to the bookshelf, grabbing a volume, only to let the book fall after he had flicked through its contents. The afternoon passed by in a confused haze.

Depressingly, that set the tone for the next three weeks. Daid remained incapable of remembering where the answer lay, although he knew that it was somewhere in one of his books. But there were so many, and although he'd read parts of all of them, and most of some of them, his erratic approach and haphazard filing system meant that he was unable to remember the book he wanted, never mind find it.

As Daid fretted, so Grandpa became ever more anxious, knowing that Hallows' Eve was a chance not to be missed. He was convinced that some of the manuscripts had been mislaid, but try as he might, he couldn't find them. Jack and Petros, aware of these concerns, felt powerless. But if Grandpa and Daid between them could not solve the problem, what chance had they?

26
Solving the Riddles

Monday arrived. Just a day to go to Hallows' Eve. Grandpa Sandy had become almost frantic. The lost manuscripts remained lost, and Daid was no nearer to finding the book he sought. The tutor had lapsed into a state of melancholy, informing the apprentices that he was unfit to live under the castle with members of the Congress.

By the time of Murkle's lesson that afternoon, a dark cloud of despondency hung over the Shian square. The rock wall crystals showered their light, but somehow it was duller than usual. Only Fenrig appeared cheery, as he recounted his planned exploits at Hallows' Eve.

"I'm going to play some really good tricks on stupid humans," he announced as they made their way to Murkle's door. "They won't know what's hit them by the time I'm finished."

Although most of the group shared a distaste for Fenrig much of the time, there was some approval for this.

"The humans are driving the animals away," said Diana heatedly. "Even the charmed places are getting smaller."

Murkle opened the door and ushered the group in. Once they were all inside, he sat in his usual chair and began to recite. Like the others, Jack had learnt by now how to cope with the tedium. He closed his eyes and pictured the woods of Keldy, then the streams in Rangie. Within minutes, Jack was miles away. Murkle occasionally gazed around the room, but he too seemed to be far away in his own world, reciting stories that should have been interesting, but which none of his class wanted to hear.

Purdy, sitting next to Jack, used his body to shield herself from Murkle. As the tutor droned on, she sat and doodled on a scrap of paper on the small area of seat between herself and Jack. Sometimes purposeful, sometimes absent-minded, she sketched away.

Murkle coughed, and Jack sat up with a start, but the teacher quickly resumed his story.

"On certain exceptional nights, the ghosts of long ago can be conjured up with the sounding of a special ram's horn. The horn may revive all those connected with a particular object or place, and unlike any other night the ghosts can act as if they were alive, but this can only be . . ."

Jack lapsed again into half-sleep as Murkle's voice droned on. Realising that there was still some way to go, Jack looked sleepily around. The other apprentices were each silently following their chosen paths of boredom relief. His mind still fuzzy from his daydream, Jack glanced down at Purdy's doodles.

She's quite artistic; they're nice patterns. Swirls and curves, knots and spirals; she's linked them up nicely.

Spirals. At the back of Jack's bored mind, a candle ignited. He looked at the paper again. There was no doubt: it was a Triple-S spiral.

He sat bolt upright, suddenly awake.

"Where did you see that?!"

There was a stir of interest around the room. Murkle looked over angrily towards Jack.

"Harrumph . . . What's the meaning of this?" he barked.

"I–I'm sorry," stammered Jack. "I saw something."

"And what is so important that you have to shout in my lesson?"

Jack was caught. He didn't want to draw attention to Purdy's drawing, especially with Fenrig looking on, but there was always a risk the others would see it anyway.

"Could I see you and Purdy outside for a minute, please, Murkle?" he asked, surreptitiously slipping his hand over Purdy's drawing.

Murkle glared at Jack for a moment, and Jack wondered briefly whether the teacher was going to beat him. Then Murkle stood up abruptly and led Jack and Purdy out of the room, closing the door. He had not reverted the youngsters to their normal size, and towered over them.

"Well?" he demanded severely.

Jack realised he had nothing to lose now.

"Please, Murkle, it's the pattern on Tamlina's ring you saw at the Congress meeting, the one you said wasn't Shian. Purdy's just drawn it."

"Thanks a bunch," muttered Purdy out of the corner of her mouth, but to her surprise Murkle did not scold her.

"Let me see," Murkle said brusquely.

"I saw it in Daid's book." Purdy handed over the drawing. "I liked some of the designs in it."

"We must show this to Atholmor," said Murkle, looking down at Jack. "I'll keep the others occupied."

He stepped out of the kitchen, but was back within half a minute.

"They won't get out. I've hexed the doorway and I've sent a grig to fetch Atholmor. Come on. Young Purdy, you'd better get that book. They'll want to examine it."

Purdy quickly retrieved the book, and Murkle carried it reverently into Jack's house, presenting it to Grandpa Sandy. Atholmor and Rowan had been summoned from a meeting in Keldy, arriving along the low road. When asked, Purdy quickly found the place from where she had copied the symbols.

"The chapter's all about the woman's visit to Dunvik," began Grandpa. "A local legend says the Cup was taken there after many years of wandering. There's quite a bit about who owned the Cup beforehand." Grandpa skimmed through the pages. "Ah, here we are. *The Cup was eventually hidden in a cave, whose exact location is a mystery. Only when the moon rises at Hallows' Eve does it reveal itself. It can be found by anyone, but only kept by those whose heart is true.*"

"But which cave, Grandpa? And what did Tamlina mean about the thief's brief reward? Or the fire and sword?"

Grandpa Sandy continued to scan the pages silently. Eventually his eyes came to rest on a particular passage, and he read it carefully. Then, turning to Purdy, he said softly, "Young Purdy, I would ask you to leave us for now. To know certain things might place you in some danger. For your own safety's sake, please step outside for a minute. You too, Jack."

Purdy pouted, but did not dare to challenge a senior Congress member. Reluctantly, she and Jack left.

"Do we have our answer?" asked Rowan expectantly.

Grandpa Sandy looked up and smiled at his old friend.

"We do. The mystery of the Cup's whereabouts is solved."

The rest of that afternoon was pandemonium. Hallows' Eve being the next day, there was little time to arrange matters. Most of the Congress seemed to be in the front room, and all were discussing the book's revelations. Daid had turned up, somewhat bleary-eyed, and was both shocked and excited to discover that his book was not lost after all.

"There's no secret about this," commented Petros as he and Jack stood outside. "Everyone in the square knows something's going on."

Out of the corner of his eye he spied Fenrig beside Mawkit's house. "If Fenrig catches on, that'll mean trouble. Let's get him."

He and Jack ran down to the foot of the square. When they got there, Fenrig was standing calmly by the back door, a short green coat slung over his shoulder. He looked at them scornfully, then casually put the coat on, and vanished.

"How'd he do that?" gasped Petros.

Jack's eyes nearly popped out of his head. This would explain why Fenrig had been so hard to track, but he knew also that Gilmore had not yet taught them how to make invisible clothes. Someone must be making them for him. This spelt trouble.

"We've got to tell Grandpa," said Jack. "Fenrig could be following us and listening in anytime."

"You're right," said Petros, and they started back to the house.

As they neared it, they could see the Congress members leaving, evidently in a hurry.

"Grandpa! We've something to tell you," shouted Petros.

"It'll have to wait," said his grandfather, hastening to catch up with Atholmor.

"But it's important, Grandpa! It's about Fenrig."

"I'm afraid we haven't time now," said Grandpa, hurrying off. "There's not a moment to lose. We must get to the Cup before the Brashat."

Jack and Petros looked on bewildered as the Congress all made haste up to the top end of the square. Rowan turned and gave a friendly wave before rushing on to catch up with the others.

"Mum, why won't they listen?" asked Petros plaintively. "We've just seen Fenrig, and he can disappear. That's dangerous."

"You'd better do what your grandfather says," answered Katie, wiping her eyes. "We'll just have to wait here until they get back." After a few moments, she went inside the house and silently climbed the stairs.

"D'you want to know where they've gone, then?" asked Rana, who had appeared at Petros's side. Jack turned to her.

"I suppose you know, then? How'd you manage that?"

"It doesn't matter how we found out," grinned Rana. "The point is, we know."

"All right, so tell us."

"What's it worth?" said Lizzie.

"Yes, what are you going to give us?" asked Purdy. "It was me who led them to the answer. We deserve something from all this."

"If you don't, I'll . . ." Petros's voice trailed off. "All right, I'll lend you my Aximon charm. Cormac made it. It's for getting you away from an attacker."

He fished inside his pocket and pulled out the small wooden figure.

"Cool," said Rana, holding out her hand.

"But you're only borrowing it," said Petros as he handed it over. "Dad'll be furious if he thinks I've given it to you. If you're in danger you say '*Salvus!*' three times, but you really have to believe in it, otherwise it's useless. Dad was firm about that. Now, what have you found out?"

"Not here," said Rana. "The esplanade. Not so many prying eyes there."

Without another word she led the way up to the esplanade gate. It was drizzling when they emerged, and Jack shivered as the fine rain settled on him.

"Dunvik's this place up on the west coast," began Rana. "There's a cave near a sea loch, with a big forest behind it. It's a long story, but the King's Cup was hidden there. It only shows itself on Hallows' Eve, when the moon rises. And get this: the Cup was made by monks."

"And d'you think the whole Congress is away up there now?" asked Jack. "Hallows' Eve is tomorrow."

"I don't fancy going all the way up there," grimaced Petros. "It's too far."

"The Congress wants to get there as soon as they can. They're scared the Brashat will beat them to it," said Rana. "Atholmor says it'll be a disaster if that happens."

"How d'you know all this?" asked Jack, at which Rana just smiled.

"We've got our ways," said Lizzie.

"Well, if you're so clever, how are you going to get up there?" asked Petros.

"I–I don't know," admitted Rana.

There was a moment of silence while she and her sister looked awkwardly at each other.

"The horses!" said Jack. "We could get them from the same place as before."

"They wouldn't know where to go." Petros was unconvinced. "And anyway, how would you get them out without being seen? Maybe we should leave it up to the Congress."

"No," said Jack firmly. "We've got to get to Dunvik." He paused. Then his eyes lit up. "Ossian can get the horses. And he might be very useful if things get dangerous."

"I don't fancy going on a horse," said Purdy. "Anyway, how can we tell him in time?"

"She's right," said Petros. "How do we get him down from Keldy?"

Jack turned to him. "The low road, of course. And you don't have to come to Dunvik if you don't want." His tone was both a challenge and a rebuke.

Petros felt his sisters' eyes boring into him.

"All right, we'll go," he mumbled.

"We can't get the horses out before it's dark, so we've got a couple of hours," Jack pointed out. "Look, I can go up to Keldy and fetch Ossian. We could be back in under an hour."

Pausing only to fetch his satchel, into which he stuffed a spare shirt and the ram's horn, Jack headed down to the gloomy garden beside Mawkit's house. As he neared the mound, he slowed down. What if Fenrig was around? Then, rationalising that he had little influence over where Fenrig was or what he was seeing, Jack resolved to carry on. Stepping onto the mound, he pulled his cloak around his face with his arms, and uttered, "Wind-flock Keldy!"

27
The Flight to Dunvik

Jack felt like he'd been pulled up in a tornado. He had never used the low road on his own before. Now he was getting its full force. He clamped his eyes shut, and within what seemed like seconds, found himself beside the oak tree at Keldy. Clouds hung low over the hills, and a misty rain made it difficult to see far.

There was no one about. Jack trotted off towards Ossian's house, but within seconds his trousers were soaked from the long wet grass. He hadn't worked out what he would do if Ossian wasn't there, and was relieved to see his cousin sitting outside. Jack approached as quietly as he could, and crouched down some twenty yards from the house.

"Psst!"

Ossian didn't appear to hear.

"Psssst!" he called again, louder and more urgently. Ossian's face looked up, and he saw his young cousin.

"Jack!" he called.

"Shhh!" hissed Jack, beckoning Ossian away from the house.

"What is it? Why're you here?"

"We have to get to Dunvik tonight. We need your help getting some horses. You know, from the place we used before."

"Dunvik's a long way. Why d'you need to go there?"

"Treasure," said Jack, figuring this was a sure way to get Ossian interested. He was right. Ossian's eyes lit up at the word, and he leaned forward earnestly.

"What kind of treasure?"

"The kind that Shian have been seeking for centuries. It's the King's Cup."

Ossian let out a low whistle. "And it's up in Dunvik? Does Cosmo know this?"

"We've only just found out ourselves. The Congress is heading up there now to be ready for Hallows' Eve. They're scared the Brashat will get there first."

"I've met Brashat before. Some of them were OK."

"Ossian, if they get hold of the Cup it means trouble. D'you know what power that will give them? Nowhere will be safe."

Ossian considered this for a moment. "All right. But the humans down near Falabray weren't as stupid as we thought. They've put iron locks on the stable doors now. We can't get past them. How many d'we need?"

"Well, there's you, me and Petros, and we'll have to take Rana and Lizzie because they found out about Dunvik."

"Three will do, then," mused Ossian. "I can manage that. But we'll need to get the others up here by dusk. That's about an hour away. Can you get them back here in that time?"

Jack nodded confidently, the excitement in him rising.

"Right. You get the others and meet me back here. Have you eaten?" Jack shook his head. "All right, I'll get some food. Mum's gettin' ready for tomorrow's party – there's loads."

By the time Jack returned an hour later with the others, Ossian was getting restless. The rain had stopped, but the evening was getting gloomy.

"I thought you'd got lost," he muttered, fingering the sack in which he had stashed some food.

"We couldn't get away," explained Petros. "Mum kept asking us questions. She knew something was up. We'd to get Purdy to call in and ask her to go next door."

"Did you see Cosmo on the road?" Ossian asked expectantly. All four shook their heads. "I sent a grig; I hope she didn't get lost."

"We should get going," said Jack, who had noted with satisfaction that the low road trip had dried out his clothes and shoes. He could enjoy these journeys now, unlike Lizzie, who remained pale and quiet.

"You'll be all right once we get up in the air. You like the horses." He patted Lizzie's arm.

Ossian led them from the oak tree and away from his house. "You and Jack take one horse," he said to Petros. "And the girls can go together. D'you feel up to that? There's reins."

"We'll be fine." Rana handed Lizzie a small satchel, which she swung over her back, tying the straps firmly in front of her.

Ossian stopped. "Are you sure it's safe to bring them?" he asked Petros.

"We can't *not* take them, they'd follow us anyway. This way I can keep an eye on them."

They mounted the horses, and with Ossian giving the signal, "Horse and hattock!" they were all soon airborne. Jack shivered as they climbed higher into the cold night air, the wind rushing past him.

"How long will it take?" he shouted, his horse pulling alongside Ossian's.

"To the north-west coast?" Ossian bellowed back. "We should make it in ten minutes."

Rana and Lizzie spurred their own horse on to join the others. Lizzie had got over her low road travel sickness, and she and Rana were both clearly enjoying the ride.

"This is great!" shouted Rana. "Look, there's a town down there."

"Never mind down there," said Petros, "you keep a tight hold of those reins." He turned and shouted across at Ossian, "Are you sure you know where we're going?"

"I went fishin' in the dark loch once," said Ossian. "Huge fish, straight in from the sea. At high tide the water sometimes reaches the cave."

"But d'you know where we're going to land?" shouted Jack.

"There's a forest behind the cave, then some fields. We'll head there."

Within minutes, Ossian was directing the horses towards the ground. Jack could see dark blurs that must have been trees, but unlike at Claville there were no landing lights tonight to direct the incoming fliers.

"Are you sure you know where the fields are?"

Ossian scanned the ground for the fields that he knew were down there somewhere. Looking up, Jack caught sight of five more horses above them, just visible in the dark sky.

"Ossian!" He pointed upwards.

"Quick! Down here!"

The horses descended quickly, skimming some treetops before coming down awkwardly in a small clearing. As they landed, each youngster rose to human height. Ossian's horse stumbled on landing, whinnying angrily, and catapulted Ossian to the side. His right leg struck a tree. Stifling an oath, he sat and rubbed his leg. Rana knelt down by the horse.

"I think she's broken her leg," she sniffed.

Ossian swore under his breath, but managed to limp over to the stunned horse. From the little light available, Jack could see fear in its eyes. Ossian knelt down stiffly and inspected the horse's leg.

"You're right. We can't do anythin' for her here. I might be able to fix this back in Keldy, but I don't have the right stones wi' me."

"But we can't just leave her here," said Lizzie, starting to cry. "She's in pain and afraid."

"I'm no' goin' to leave her in pain," said Ossian.

Still kneeling down beside the horse, he caressed her trembling neck, moving both hands soothingly up and down the beast's collar. The horse's eyes slowly closed, and its breathing settled. Ossian reached into his pocket and withdrew a small phial, and poured a little oil into the horse's ear. The horse went suddenly rigid, then lay limp.

"You've killed her!" exclaimed Rana.

"I've stopped her pain." Ossian looked hard at Rana. "I couldn't fix her leg here. And she may no' be the last one to die. Who saw where those other horses went? Do we know who was on them?"

❧ 187 ❧

"I'll bet it was the Brashat," stated Jack. "Somehow they'll have found out where we've gone."

Ossian led the two horses away into the woods and tied them up where they couldn't see their dead stablemate.

"We missed the fields, didn't we?" sniffed Lizzie. "D'you know where we are?"

"We can't be far from Dunvik, but it was too dark to see properly. The moon didn't help much."

As if to mock the youngsters, the clouds now parted, allowing the moonlight to shine through.

"That's typical," muttered Ossian. "Well, whoever they were we can only hope they didn't see us. Now, we need to find some runnin' water. This way, and stick together. I don't want anyone wanderin' off."

Bowing to Ossian's superior knowledge of woodlands, Jack and the others fell into step behind him. It was a long time, however, before he found a small stream.

"How d'you know it was here?" asked Lizzie.

"Sometimes you feel it runnin' beneath you," said Ossian. "But there's no knowin' where it'll surface."

Kneeling down again with difficulty, Ossian took a small pouch from his waist and extracted three pebbles.

"I thought you said you didn't have any stones with you," said Rana.

"These aren't the healin' kind. They're my compass," replied Ossian irritably.

He quickly cleared a small area in the undergrowth and leant over to the stream to moisten one of the pebbles. Then, holding all three together in his right hand, he threw them as if they were dice.

"The wet pebble's a sea stone, that one's a wood stone, and this is granite. They show where the cave and the forest are, and where the sea is. We must have over-shot the fields. The cave's over there," he indicated the way they had come. "We'd better get goin'."

"Those other horses went further than we did," pointed out Jack. "They must have overshot the fields too."

"You're right," said Ossian. "We may still get there first."

"What's in Dunvik apart from the cave?" asked Petros.

"No' much. There were some human villages, but they got cleared ages ago."

"'Cleared'?" asked Rana.

"The people got shipped away, to Canada or America. All they left were graveyards, and a lot of sheep. But this isn't really Shian territory. That's why we're human height here."

"So humans got banished as well?" asked Jack. "It's not just the Shian who got pushed around?"

"Some o' them," grunted Ossian. "Some o' the ones doin' the pushin' were pretty bad, though. It's hard to like them when you see what they did to their own kind, never mind us."

"So, some humans are all right then?"

"Of course," snapped Ossian. "But some deserve everythin' they get."

They walked on in silence, Ossian still limping. The air was clear and fresh. Lizzie, shivering as quietly as she could, pulled her cloak tightly around her.

After a while, Ossian held up his hand, and they all halted. "Shhh!"

There was no doubt about it: there were voices ahead. The five crouched down, trying hard to hold their breath.

❀ 189 ❀

"I can't make out who it is," hissed Ossian. "Someone'll have to go closer and find out. With this leg I'd make too much noise."

"We'll do it," chorused Rana and Lizzie.

"I meant Jack or Petros," replied Ossian coldly.

"We've something that'll help us," explained Rana. "Show him, Lizzie."

Lizzie unhooked her satchel and took out two small green bonnets.

"Are they what I think they are?" whispered Jack. "How'd you get them?"

"Freya made them," said Rana. "You thought Fenrig was the only one stealing cloths? Freya's been making charmed clothes for ages."

"You wore them when we went to see Tamlina, didn't you?" exclaimed Petros, half in awe, half in anger.

"Never mind that now," hissed Ossian. "Can you get close enough to find out who they are?"

"'Course we can." Rana placed the bonnet on her head. "Look. Or you could try looking, but you can't see." She couldn't resist laughing at the expression on Petros's face.

"Would you keep quiet?!" hissed Ossian. "This isn't a joke. If others are after the King's Cup, they'll no' take kindly to us bein' here."

Rana and Lizzie fell silent, and, invisible to the eye, moved off carefully towards the sound of voices. Jack sat down, his heart thumping. It nearly leapt up his throat a few minutes later when a voice beside him said, "Boo!"

A peal of laughter echoed through the woods as Rana and Lizzie took off their bonnets.

"That's not funny!" yelled Jack.

"Oh yes it was," said Rana. "It's OK, it's Grandpa and some of the Congress. They've made a fire."

"Did they see you?" asked Ossian.

"'Course not, we're not stupid," replied Lizzie. "Grandpa'll be pleased to see us. They've got a fire going. You don't see it until you're up close."

"Well, you're making enough noise," hissed Petros. "They're bound to have heard you by now."

He was right. Without warning a beam of light illuminated the whole area, blinding them.

"Stand up, and put your hands on top of your heads," commanded a voice. The five obeyed.

"Grandpa, it's us," shouted Rana, her eyes tightly closed.

Jack felt his hands being seized and quickly tied behind his back, while a hood was placed over his head. To his left he heard Lizzie complaining that 'that was sore'. The five, hooded and stumbling, were made to walk by rough prods in the back. Their captors, whoever they were, did not speak. Jack thought he recognised the Darrig's distinctive smell.

"Ow!" shouted Rana. "Quit it, will you?"

"That's far enough!" the same voice directed them.

Jack's hood was taken from his head, and he faced the bright beam of light again. Gradually the light dimmed, and slowly he was able to open his eyes. As they became accustomed to the light, he saw his Uncle Doonya standing in front of him.

"Dad!" exclaimed Lizzie, but her greeting did not get the expected reply.

"What the hell are you kids doing here?"

28
The Dunvik Oak

The youngsters sat huddled while the Congress members discussed their fate. They were too far away from the fire to feel its warmth, but near enough to hear that the conversation was heated. None felt like speaking, and they sat, cold and disconsolate.

After a while, Grandpa Sandy and Doonya approached, the stone from Grandpa's sceptre lighting up their faces.

"Ossian," said Grandpa sternly, "you know better than to risk the lives of your cousins, Rana and Lizzie in particular. You shall return to Keldy at first light."

The group sat, mute, avoiding eye contact in the dim light.

"You should all be close to home, especially on Hallows' Eve. Jack, I thought I had impressed on you the danger of being so far from the safety of the castle."

"We thought we could help," said Jack quietly. "We discovered things about the Cup and the spirals, and we know there's others here too – we saw five horses above us."

"We saw them too," replied Doonya crossly. "That should remind you of the danger. Didn't you realise you might be followed? That you might lead the Brashat here?"

"Dad, the Brashat know more than you think." Petros's voice was plaintive. "We tried to tell you earlier. Fenrig can disappear. He could have overheard everything."

"Gilmore said some charmed cloth had been stolen. But how did Fenrig make that into clothes?" asked Grandpa.

Rana and Lizzie looked uneasily at each other, but neither spoke.

"We don't know," answered Jack. "But he could've been eavesdropping for ages. Is the whole Congress here?"

"Just Atholmor, Rowan, Finbogie, and the Darrig. The others will come tomorrow." Grandpa paused and looked at the youngsters. Lizzie had started shivering. "You had better come and sit by the fire. Don't worry, it's charmed, it can't be seen more than twenty yards away. And tomorrow morning you are all going home."

"Are we far from the cave, Grandpa?" asked Rana as they walked towards the small clearing.

"It's a couple of hundred yards away. Tomorrow we shall be in the best place to find the Cup. We're camped by the old hermit's cell," continued Grandpa. "There's little of it left now. About half a mile over there," he indicated with his arm, "is an old ruined castle that belonged to the lord of these parts. An evil man; he cleared his own people away."

"But what if the Brashat come?" asked Jack.

"Tomorrow is Hallows' Eve, a day sacred for all Shian creatures. Even the Brashat would not dare to break that."

"Are you sure?" asked Jack uncertainly.

"I'm sure, but I still don't want you young ones getting mixed up with the Brashat. Hallows' Eve is a day for celebration, when we look back and honour all those who have gone before us." Grandpa examined the stone in his sceptre. "It's late. Time you lot got some sleep."

He indicated a flattish bit of ground near the fire, and the five youngsters settled down. Sleep did not come easily, however. The ground was hard, the night cold and a constant muttering came from the Congress members around the fire. It was some time before Jack and the others drifted off.

Jack woke with a start. It was still dark, the fire having all but died out. Someone was tugging his arm.

"Get up!" hissed Ossian. "And be quiet."

"What is it?" asked Jack blearily.

"Shhh! Come wi' me."

Jack looked over to the fire. The Congress members were all asleep, either propped against a tree, or curled up on the ground. Ossian silently woke the others, and together they all crept away from the camp. When they had gone about fifty yards, Ossian stopped.

"A Ghillie-Doo warned me," he whispered. "There's Brashat and Hobshee swarmin' all over the forest."

"We have to warn Grandpa, then," said Jack.

"He won't listen. You heard him last night. He's just goin' to send us packin'."

"What do we do, then?" whispered Rana.

"We'll have to hide. The Cup only shows itself when the moon rises."

"What time's it now?" asked Lizzie, simultaneously yawning and shivering.

"Dawn's not far off," replied Ossian. "We'll hole up for the day, then see how we can help when evenin' comes."

"Where's safe if there's Brashat and Hobshee all around?" asked Jack.

"There's an old oak. It's got this huge cavern in its trunk. I sheltered there once before; the rain was lashin' down, but it was a fine shelter. It's no' too far."

The first glows of daylight were lightening the sky. Jack yawned as Ossian led them along a faint path. Sure enough, not two hundred yards away, there was an oak tree. Ducking under a low hanging branch, Ossian crawled through a tear in the bark, followed by the others. It was dry inside, and felt a lot warmer than being out in the open.

"It's pitch dark," complained Rana.

Tutting, Ossian extracted a small stone from his pouch and set it down. Muttering inaudibly, he flicked his fingers at the stone, and it began to glow. Though dim, they could see that there was room inside for them all.

"We'll take turns watchin'," said Ossian. "I'll go first. You lot get some rest."

Over the next few hours Ossian, Jack and Petros took it in turns to watch. Against his better judgement, Ossian allowed Rana and Lizzie to go out for a while with their green bonnets on. They returned quickly, however, having seen figures moving among the trees.

"D'you see who they were?" asked Ossian.

"We didn't get close enough," replied Rana. "It wasn't the Congress, though."

"I want to go home," said Lizzie. "And I'm hungry."

"I brought some food wi' me."

As Ossian and Petros laid out the provisions they'd brought, Jack edged round so that he was closer to Ossian.

Being cooped up in here's bad enough, but Aunt Katie's food will make it desperate. At least Aunt Dorcas can cook.

"What can we do if there's Brashat and Hobshee around?" Lizzie's voice trembled.

"We have to get into the cave," said Jack. "The Cup's in there somewhere. The Congress can't complain if we help them get it."

"D'you want a bet?" said Petros. "Dad's going to be furious, whatever happens."

"We'll have to face that when it happens," reasoned Jack. "The important thing's to get the Cup before the Brashat."

"Atholmor said if the Brashat get the Cup, it could make them so strong they'll challenge us for the square in Edinburgh," stated Rana. "And then they'd get the Stone."

"How are we all goin' to get to the cave? There'll be Congress members and Brashat all over the place," said Ossian.

"Lizzie and me can use our bonnets," said Rana. "And we brought along some others too."

"What other ones?" demanded Petros.

"A shifter," said Rana airily, "and a beetler."

"You've never got a beetler, have you?" exclaimed Jack. *A cap that shrinks you to the size of a beetle! How cool is that?*

Rana smiled smugly. "How d'you think I heard what the Congress was talking about yesterday?" she said. "Freya's been very busy, and she's a good friend."

"Freya showed me the shifter while she was making it," said Jack. "It's brilliant."

"You can have it, then, and Petros can take the beetler," announced Lizzie.

"Well, that gets three of us into the cave, I guess," said Jack. "But crawling all the way could take hours. And anyone might step on you."

Petros's face registered his disgust at the thought.

"I'll manage," said Ossian confidently. "The Brashat won't be lookin' for me, anyway."

"Maybe we should hand this back to the Congress," said Petros apprehensively. "I want to go back to Edinburgh."

"We'll go together," said Jack firmly. "How're you going to get back to Edinburgh, anyway? You can take the beetler when we get near the cave. Once we get inside we'll just have to play it by ear."

Petros grunted, but didn't reply.

The tree trunk's cavernous interior was home to many creatures other than the five youngsters. However, Petros and Jack had no luck in trying to get earwigs to run races, and Lizzie announced that she detested staying in a place with so many spiders.

By mid-afternoon, Petros had gravitated to kicking the inside of the trunk in sheer frustration, leading to a short but heated argument with Jack about how best to give themselves away. Rana and Lizzie had ventured outside again using their bonnets, but had seen no one. Ossian cautioned them against straying too far.

"We have to keep an element o' surprise," he said. "Showin' ourselves too early could ruin everythin'."

"This is the dullest Hallows' Eve ever," said Lizzie after a long pause. "We should be out playing tricks, not stuck in a tree with spiders."

"I bet Purdy and Freya are having fun now," said Rana moodily. "They'll be up on the esplanade, or doing all sorts down the High Street."

"Let's tell stories, then, or have some songs," said Jack. "Who knows any good ones about Hallows' Eve?"

"I've got one," said Ossian, and he began:

> *Witchie-hags shall come, shall come,*
> *And demons will be in among,*
> *While Shian tricks will tease Dameve*
> *All on the night of Hallows' Eve.*

"I thought you said you didn't mind some of the humans," said Rana angrily. "Why d'you call them that?"

"I've met some bad ones. They don't care for where they live; they poison the water and the plants. And they think they're so smart."

"You really don't like them, do you?" said Lizzie.

"They don't even like each other," said Ossian heatedly. "You look at this place, Dunvik. There used to be three or four villages near here. Now there's no people, they all got driven away. Keldy's the same. And the ones you do meet, they're so noisy." He paused for breath, but Rana butted in before he could continue.

"Well, Mum's dad was a human. That makes us a quarter human, so you'd better watch what you say, Ossian."

"I don't hate all o' them," muttered Ossian.

"Let's change the subject, shall we?" said Petros.

The five fell silent, and for a while nothing was said.

The light outside started to dim, and suddenly the interior of the tree was infested with small midges. The youngsters swiped away at them, but it made little difference.

"Can't we burn something to get rid of them?" asked Lizzie, which drew a withering look from her brother.

"We'll head out in fifteen minutes," said Ossian. "It'll still be light enough to see."

The next quarter of an hour dragged by. Like the others, Jack had become thoroughly fed up. The tree's interior seemed to be closing in on him, and he longed to get out and stretch his legs properly. As yet more birds returned home to the tree to settle for the night, Ossian finally decided that it was safe for them to leave.

29
Hallows' Eve

Rana and Lizzie were first out, trusting in their bonnets. They crept back to the camp, but found no one. Rana took her bonnet off, turned back and indicated this to the boys, then she and Lizzie carried on. Above the sound of a few chattering birds, Ossian whispered that he would make a tour of the nearby forest before meeting up with the others close to the cave. Jack and Petros nodded agreement, and set off after the girls. Cautiously, they followed the path downwards.

"Where's the cave, then?"

"Ossian said it overlooked the dark loch. The water's over that way – the cave must be nearby." Then Jack paused. The muscles beside his eyes were twitching furiously, and he was aware that the birdsong had ceased.

"Why's it so quiet?" he whispered. "What's happened to the birds?"

Petros stopped and listened. "You're right. Something's frightened them off."

Thwack!

A flinthead arrow shot past Jack's face, embedding itself in a tree behind him. On impulse, both boys began to run. Petros was furiously trying to retrieve something from his pocket. In seconds, he had pulled out a dark purple cloth and placed it over his head. Instantly he shrank down out of sight.

The beetler cloth, of course!

Jack had no option but to continue, although he had little idea of where he was heading.

Reaching a large yew tree, he ducked behind it, gasping for breath. After a minute, the thumping in his chest quietened and his breathing settled. Straining, he listened for any sound that might be his pursuer. Nothing. Cautiously, he peered out.

Zap!

The hex lifted him bodily from the ground. Struggling to turn his head, Jack saw with relief that Rowan from the Congress was standing ten yards away, holding his sceptre up.

"Well, well, so we find you at last," said Rowan calmly. "You have been a slippery little boy. And where are your cousins?"

"I don't know," gasped Jack.

"You're lying!" shouted Rowan. Then, collecting himself, he said, "We'd better take you to join the Congress."

He lowered his sceptre, breaking the hex. Jack fell to the ground, landing on his satchel.

Relieved that he would at least see Grandpa and Uncle Doonya, Jack gratefully got up. Rowan shoved him in the back and Jack stumbled forwards.

"Not far to go now," taunted Rowan after a few minutes. The sound of the water was louder, and Jack could feel rock breaking through the forest floor.

The cave must be near.

And then Jack's blood almost froze. From behind a tree stepped a Hobshee. Short, a malevolent grin spread across its face, it leered at Jack. He turned to Rowan who, to his amazement, just smiled. Rowan shoved Jack again, and he fell forward down the slope. Picking himself up, Jack saw more Hobshee milling around. He could smell roasting meat too.

"Here we are!" said Rowan with malicious satisfaction. "Now you can join the rest of your family!"

Jack stepped around the rock and saw that it was the side of the cave entrance. And there in the gloom, huddled together with their backs to the opposite wall, were the members of the Congress. Jack blinked disbelievingly. His grandfather, grimacing in obvious pain, had a gash above his eye. They all looked cowed, beaten, but why? Jack took a step forward and got his answer. Several Brashat, Briannan among them, were aiming sceptres at the prisoners. For that undoubtedly is what they were. Dazed, Jack stumbled forward. Grandpa Sandy looked up, but made no sound.

"Ah, I wondered how long it would be before these meddlesome youngsters showed up," crowed Briannan. "I trust that you have brought all your wretched friends with you?"

Jack looked imploringly at his grandfather. Then he noticed a small fire at the side of the cave, above which sausages were crackling and spitting on a griddle. Despite the appetising aroma, Jack saw to his disgust that Fenrig was the cook. Jack clenched his fists and moved instinctively towards his antagonist, but he got no further. A bolt from Briannan's sceptre caught him square in the chest. He staggered back, gasping, a searing pain in his lungs.

"I can see that you will have to learn the hard way, like your interfering grandfather," said Briannan coldly.

He motioned to another Brashat, who stepped forward and picked Jack up by the arm, shoving him roughly towards his uncle. Briannan then turned and mocked the Congress.

"My young Fenrig found the invisibility tailoring we taught him most valuable: all those conversations about lost treasures . . . quite the little spy, isn't he?"

As Fenrig smirked under his father's praise, a hoodie crow flew into the cave, settling on his extended left forearm. Soundlessly, it opened its beak and deposited a tiny beetle onto Fenrig's left palm. The bird hopped off onto the ground, instantly transforming into a young woman of fifteen or sixteen.

"Thank you, Morrigan," drawled Briannan. Seeing Jack's look of astonishment, he continued, "I don't believe you've met Fenrig's sister, have you?"

Morrigan preened herself. Jack recognised her from the midsummer festival. She was undeniably pretty – her eyes were gorgeous – but she had the same smugness and condescension exhibited by her brother.

"Now, what shall we do with this insignificant beetle?" sneered Fenrig, making as if to clap his hands.

"No!" shouted Jack, finally getting his breath back.

Fenrig held his right hand just a couple of inches above his left, on which the tiny beetle scuttled, never daring to go over the edge.

"In view of the auspicious nature of this day, I think we will be gracious to our young captive."

Fenrig dropped the insect, which transfigured back into Petros as it hit the ground. The youngster sat up, bewildered and scared. Doonya crouched down, beckoning Petros to join him.

"That beetler disguise is the worst move I ever made," he muttered to Jack. "I thought that bird was going to eat me. Bloody terrifying. And her breath smelt foul."

Rowan stepped forward, his sceptre held at waist level, pointing at the prisoners.

"And you, Rowan," Petros's fear turned to anger, "to betray the Congress."

"The Congress is finished. It's weak. It was dragging the whole Shian people down into the mire. Now we will have strong leadership, and the Shian will rise again."

Uncle Doonya gripped the shoulders of Jack and Petros. Jack realised with a sinking feeling that none of the Congress could speak, and now Grandpa Sandy slumped against the cave wall. At first, Jack thought he had fainted, but then he saw that his grandfather was watching the sky out of the mouth of the cave. Briannan stepped forward.

"See, the moon rises. Soon the Cup will be revealed, and the Brashat will know the secrets of life and death!"

Everyone turned to gaze at the moon as it made its way above some trees beyond the cave. Its light was weak, the night not yet being truly dark, but an eerie glow filled the mouth of the cave. Briannan turned round sharply and extinguished the griddle fire with a bolt from his sceptre. He stared at the back of the cave.

"Where does the light fall? Where is the Cup?"

Gradually, a corner at the rear of the cave began to smoulder, and a few flames flickered. The Hobshee retreated, their yelping cries betraying their fear of the unknown. Briannan, with no such qualms, strode forwards. Plunging his hand into the base of the flames, he grasped the Cup. Withdrawing it in triumph, he turned round and brandished the prize. Though tarnished and covered in cobwebs and grime, the Cup still glimmered.

"The King's Cup!" he proclaimed triumphantly. "Now is the time for the Unseelie to take control! Amadan will surely reward us for this."

Jack saw Atholmor wilt as they all beheld Briannan in his triumph. Grandpa, still slumped on the ground, looked pale. His mouth moved, but no sound came out. Doonya sat, transfixed, as everyone watched Briannan stride out of the cave. The flames had died down, and the cave suddenly seemed very dark. Realising that this might give the prisoners some notion of escape, Rowan twirled his sceptre and stuck it in the ground, spreading a bright glow over the front of the cave. The prisoners squinted at the sudden illumination. The returning Hobshee sneered, taunting the prisoners with mocking cries. Though small in stature, they more than made up for this in menace. Jack shrank from them as they approached.

"I think in honour of our great victory – a most auspicious night on which to triumph – we might allow these wretches their voices back," said Briannan, clearly delighted with his prize. "Konan, keep watch on them. They may speak, but not leave the cave. We'll go back to the hermit's cell."

A figure Jack knew he'd seen before now stepped into the cave, his face disfigured as if by fire. A chill swept through Jack, and he felt sick. As Briannan left to examine the Cup in more detail, Konan shuffled awkwardly forward, sceptre in hand. His eyes came to rest on Jack, and they narrowed. The chill in Jack's bones became a frost.

"You," said Konan with difficulty, his mouth tracing the words with effort, "you are the upstart pup of Phineas. You have his eyes. He caused this," he indicated his disfigured face, "before we met the Grey. Nine icy years before I escaped. Ha! I mastered time there."

With what might have been half a smile, he patted one of his pockets before scowling again.

"But I live as an outcast. When this night is done, I shall send you to join your father in his frozen tomb."

Konan stepped back. The talking had quickly tired him.

"Now you may speak. But if you try to escape, I'll kill you. And the Hobshee would welcome the chance to celebrate Hallows' Eve with some flesh." He sat back on a ledge of rock, keeping his sceptre trained on the prisoners.

"Jack, Petros, are you all right?" Grandpa spoke slowly, his voice frail.

Jack smiled weakly, and Petros hugged his grandfather.

"We're OK. How about you?"

"Briannan was showing off," mumbled Grandpa. "He caught me a blow on the head."

"But how'd they capture you?" asked Jack apprehensively. "You must've been here before them. Didn't you see them coming?"

"Rowan betrayed us," said Doonya. "He removed the charm around the fire. It was easy then for the Brashat and Hobshee to sneak up. But where are the girls? Did you send them home?"

"No, Dad. They're around somewhere – so's Ossian. They must be all right, otherwise they'd have been brought here too."

"Tell him about the bonnets, Petros."

"They've got invisible bonnets. I think Freya made them. They're smart enough to keep out of harm's way."

"I hope you're right," muttered Doonya. "I can't imagine what your mother's thinking now."

Jack nudged Petros, and indicated Konan.

"He's the one who tried to grab me back in Edinburgh," he whispered.

"You sure?"

Petros looked panicked, and Jack thought he'd leave the subject for now.

"Briannan's forgotten the Hobshee are inland creatures. They don't like the sea." Grandpa winced and clenched his teeth. "And there's a rip tide coming. I can hear it."

Jack could see that some of the Hobshee were glancing apprehensively around. The sound of the sea *was* growing in intensity.

The tide runs into this cave! Briannan's left us to drown here!

One of the Hobshee uttered a grunt and made to climb up the slope towards the hermit's cell. Two more followed, leaving just two by the cave. Distracted by this, Konan went to give them orders to remain.

Jack saw his chance. Reaching into his satchel, he retrieved the silk shifter Rana had given him back at the oak tree. Gripping his satchel, he surreptitiously placed the cap on his head just as Konan turned back towards the prisoners.

Whish!

Jack was hoiked fifteen yards outside the mouth of the cave. He fell on his side, but was quickly up and running as fast as he could. He heard shouts and curses behind him as Konan reprimanded the Hobshee.

The sea. They'll never follow me there.

Jack ran towards the sound of the water. His heart was pounding, but he knew he had to keep going. The shouts behind him grew dimmer as the noise of the waves before him became louder. At last, rounding a clump of rocks, he saw in front of him the great dark loch of Dunvik.

30
Counter-Attack

Exhausted, Jack collapsed behind a large rock. Terrified that his gasps for air could be heard half a mile away, he tried to hold his breath, and listened for the sound of pursuers. He didn't dare to look out from behind his rock.

As his body recovered from the exertion and the terror, Jack began to think. His impulse had been to get away. The memory of Konan's menacing eyes and his threats to kill the prisoners set Jack's heart racing again. He had escaped on impulse, but where could he go?

Jack looked out over the dark loch. The moon shone brightly now, its light reflecting on the ruffled waters. The waves were lapping at his feet. Ossian had said that the sea sometimes even ran into the cave.

That means this rock will be under water soon. I can't stay here long. But where do I go now? I wish Petros was here, or Grandpa.

Jack shivered. The wind was starting to whip around him now, and his body was cooling down quickly. He pulled his coat tighter around himself, but it made little difference.

I'd almost be better off in the cave, at least it's sheltered there.

Realising that he would have to make a move, Jack was debating which way to go when he heard a twig snap behind him. He froze again. Someone *had* followed him. *Well,* he thought, *it's either drown or die on my feet.* He stood up, and stepped out from behind his sheltering place.

"Hiya, Jack," said Cosmo casually. "How're you doing?"

"You could see me?" said Jack. "But how? It's dark."

"My oscuroscope. I'll tell you about it later if there's time. But first I've got to ask you: has Briannan really got the Chalice?"

"The Cup? Yes, he's taken it up to the hermit's cell."

"Damn! It's going to be hard now for us to get it back."

"Who's 'us'?"

"I've got some friends with me. Look Jack, the Cup's proper name is the Chalice. Do you know what it really is?"

"I know it's one of the three treasures. We've got the Stone in the castle. Or the humans have got it. But if we get the Cup ... I mean the Chalice, that'll make the Stone stronger. They say it tells secrets of life and death." Jack thought for a few moments. "You know all about the Cup, then?"

Cosmo just smiled. "Used properly, Jack, the Chalice could double or even treble the power of the Stone. And with the Sphere – who knows?"

"But you told the Congress you didn't know much."

"I didn't trust them. And it looks like I was right. There's a traitor, isn't there? The Brashat could never have outwitted the whole Congress."

Jack looked down. "Rowan gave them away."

"It's just as well I didn't say much then, isn't it?"

Jack could only agree, but this still didn't help them to rescue Petros and the others.

"Come on," said Cosmo. "We'll go and join my friends. Then we'll have to decide what we can do."

Together they walked around the shoreline, eventually reaching an old cottage by the water's edge. As they neared it, Jack could clearly hear Rana.

"We were doing fine! Those stupid Brashat couldn't see us. We could've got to Grandpa and the others if you'd let us."

"I'm no' goin' over this again," said Ossian in exasperation. Then he looked up. "Hiya, Jack! Cosmo find you all right?"

"How many Brashat are there?" asked Oobit, emerging from the doorway.

"Dozens," replied Jack. "And Konan had some Hobshee with him by the cave, and more went off with Briannan."

"The plan kind of centred around getting to the Chalice first," admitted Cosmo.

"But many people believe the Cup is theirs." Henri spoke up for the first time. Jack had not seen him in the gloom.

"Before we can decide where it goes, we have to get it back," replied Cosmo. "Are you with us?"

"Cosmo, you asked me as a friend, and I honour you for this," said Henri. "We are proud to join you as your allies tonight."

Allies! Jack's mind raced. Where had he heard that before? Of course! Tamlina had said the ram's horn would summon allies in the quest. Jack felt in his satchel. There it was, wrapped up in his spare shirt. And there was something else, deep down in his memory ... He frowned in concentration, gritting his teeth as he tried to remember.

"What's the matter, Jack?" asked Rana. "You look like you've just signed up for extra lessons with Murkle!"

"That's it!" shouted Jack. "Murkle's lesson – when Purdy drew the spirals! The ghosts can be conjured up with a ram's horn."

Reaching into his satchel, Jack withdrew the horn.

"Where'd you get that?" gasped Cosmo incredulously. "D'you know what it is?"

Jack hesitated. "It ... it's for summoning allies in the quest for the Cup. Tamlina gave it to me."

"Jack, that's a vococorn. If Tamlina gave you that, then you're meant to summon the monks who made the Chalice. And they have powers that we can only imagine."

Putting the horn to his lips, Jack blew steadily. For a while, nothing happened. Then a low murmuring sound reverberated around the woods, a single note that grew louder as it carried out across the water. Echoing off the rocks at the far side, it got louder still. Lizzie put her hands over her ears, vainly trying to shut out the din. Louder, and louder. Earsplitting. And then, suddenly, it stopped. The stillness of the night was almost deafening.

A series of yelps came from the direction of the cave.

"The Hobshee," said Cosmo. "They know something's up, but they won't know what's hit them when it comes."

"And what *is* coming?" asked Jack, unsure he really wanted to know.

"I told you: the ghosts of the monks."

"And they're our allies?"

212

Cosmo nodded. "They'll be here soon. And everyone, stay calm. They can be a bit unsettling. We'll go round to where I found Jack. That's the nearest point to the cave. They'll hit land there."

Cosmo set off briskly, then paused while the others caught up.

"I should've checked: who's got weapons?"

The Claville and Cos-Howe boys brandished sceptres, while Ossian lifted up a large club for inspection. Jack shook his head.

"Maybe you'd better stay out of the way, then," said Cosmo. "You take care of Rana and Lizzie."

"We can look after ourselves," said Rana indignantly. "We were fine until Ossian dragged us away."

"Yes, but the fightin's about to get fierce," said Ossian, "and you don't have any weapons."

"Look, you three stick with me and Ossian. We'll go to the cave," said Cosmo. "Henri can take the others to the hermit's cell and start on Briannan's mob."

There was no further time for discussion. A mighty whistling sound came from the sea end of the dark loch. In the distance, three white sails could be seen, one much nearer than the others. An urgent chanting sound accompanied by a steady drum rhythm carried over the water.

"What's that they're chanting?" asked Jack.

"Oh, it's not them that's chanting. That's the wind. It's Gosol," said Cosmo quietly. "You're going to see a different kind of power tonight. Get ready."

31
Ships Sail in the Forest

The first boat hit the shore just yards away, but it didn't stop. As it glided over the land, Jack, wide-eyed, could see about a dozen bareheaded figures in long grey robes, facing forward. One carried a large book, a second beat a drum and one figure at the back chimed a large bell. It sounded as if they were chanting in unison, but Jack couldn't see their mouths move.

The second and third boats were still some way from the shore. Instructing the Claville and Cos-Howe boys to wait for them, Cosmo sprinted after the first boat as it skimmed over the ground.

"Come on, then!" shouted Ossian.

Rana and Lizzie took off, and Jack set off after them. Within two minutes they could see the cave, but there was no sign of the prisoners. As the boat came to rest, the chanting and drumming stopped, but the bell continued to chime.

Konan and the Hobshee had gone, but three Brashat stood there defiantly, sceptres in hand.

"Give up!" Cosmo shouted, brandishing his sceptre. "If you surrender, no harm will come to you."

"One of you against us!" one of them snorted, while the others hooted derisively.

At that moment Ossian, Jack, Rana and Lizzie arrived.

"Five of us!" shouted Rana triumphantly.

This proclamation did not have the intended effect. A bolt from one of the Brashat sceptres flew to the top of Rana's shoulder, knocking her to the ground. As she fell, screaming in pain, howls of ridicule came from the Brashat.

One of the figures stepped over the side of the boat. He was, as Jack had thought, clad from head to foot in a grey robe, his bare head so pale that it was almost transparent. He appeared to glide towards the three Brashat, who backed away, but the figure was moving much too fast for them. As he reached the first one, he drew from within his robe a long iron sword. In a flash he had sliced into the first Brashat's midriff. Blood gushed out of the wound, and the Brashat fell. The others howled, falling back in a blind panic.

"It's iron!" yelped one.

They were scrabbling over each other, trying to get out of the way, and within seconds had disappeared.

"Amazin'!" exclaimed Ossian, advancing on the figure.

"You can't!" shouted Cosmo. "His sword is iron. He can come to you, not the other way round."

Sure enough, Ossian was halted several yards from the figure, whose blood-dripping sword hung from his hand, his face impassive. Ossian was blocked.

Rana sat up, sobbing. Boldly, Lizzie stepped towards the figure, despite Cosmo's urgent hiss to stay back. But unlike Ossian, she got to within a yard of the figure before she encountered an invisible wall. Realising that she would get no further, she simply looked up at the figure.

"Thank you."

He bowed his head slightly, but his face remained expressionless. He glided back to the boat, allowing Lizzie to run towards the cave.

"There they are!" she shouted in triumph.

Jack bounded after her, leaving Rana, wincing in pain, on the ground.

Jack and Lizzie reached the cave and ran joyfully towards the prisoners lying in its dim recess. Quickly removing their gags, the youngsters untied the prisoners. Even in the gloomy light, Jack could see the look of distress on his grandfather's face.

He looks so much older.

"Typical shoddy Hobshee," muttered Atholmor, feeling the corners of his mouth, which bled slightly. "Using a dirty human move like that. No finesse."

Doonya, on his knees, hugged Lizzie. The tiny Darrig, standing at his full height, scowled fiercely.

"Are you . . . all right?" Grandpa's voice was little more than a whisper.

"Never mind us. How are you?" said Jack anxiously.

"I've been . . . better . . . We can't . . . thank you enough."

"Yeah, nice one, Jack," said Petros, in an effort at nonchalance.

"It was the men in the boats who really helped," said Jack excitedly. "I called them with the horn Tamlina gave me. Come and see them."

Grandpa Sandy followed the others to the mouth of the cave with difficulty. The boat stood on the floor of the forest, the silent figures inside it, erect, impassive. The second and third boats had reached the water's edge now and started to skim over the ground as the first had done. Oobit, Radge and the others ran alongside.

"We need to get going," explained Cosmo. "We must get the Chalice."

Jack walked over to Rana and put his arm around her.

"Ouch!" she yelped. "My shoulder's sore, you idiot."

Jack had no time to respond. As if from nowhere, Konan had sprung up and grabbed the two of them, pinning them to his body with his huge left forearm. With his right arm he brandished his sceptre at Cosmo and the members of the Congress, who had all moved instinctively forward.

"Back off!" he shouted, his words still edged with pain. "Or I'll kill them both!"

"No!" shouted Doonya, moving forward. "Take me. Let them go."

"You'd think I'd fall for that trick?" sneered Konan. "They're my way out of here. Now stay back, or I'll snap their necks."

Rana whimpered as Doonya continued to advance slowly. Her shoulder felt as if it was burning. Jack searched his pocket frantically, and soon grasped the small wooden figure there. He whispered out of the corner of his mouth, "Aximon! Say the words with me."

Rana looked blank for a moment. Then, remembering, she fished hurriedly in her own pocket and grasped the Aximon figure Petros had lent her.

"*Salvus! Salvus! Salvus!*"

Konan's grasp slackened, and Jack and Rana were able to wriggle free of his arm. As Konan's sceptre fell to the ground, Jack grasped it and flicked it up, shouting, "Uncle Doonya!"

Doonya caught the sceptre and aimed it straight at Konan, who stood limp, his eyes glazed. Jack hurled himself out of the way.

"Not death!" shouted a voice from behind.

Jack looked up to see Cosmo advancing, slowly and carefully.

"Not death, Pierre. The power of Gosol, remember."

Doonya stared hard at Konan. He wanted to exterminate the creature who had just threatened to kill his daughter, and yet ... and yet ...

"Does Gosol really want this creature to live?" he yelled.

"A hex, yes," said Cosmo, "but you must not kill him. It is not up to us to carry that out."

Jack saw his uncle tighten his grip on the sceptre, then he fired off a bolt, and Konan's body rose from the ground, completely limp. It floated back to a large oak tree, and slowly Konan's body was absorbed into its great trunk. Doonya let the sceptre drop. There was a moment of silence. Then he ran over to Rana and clasped her to his chest, sobbing.

The second and third boats arrived and came to rest by the first. Atholmor stepped forward and went to speak to the lead figure in the first boat. His words, however, had no effect. The figure stood, impassive, facing the front of his boat. Cosmo came forward.

"He can't hear you," he explained. "He's a ghost, a memory."

"But you spoke to him," pointed out Atholmor, "and he used a sword. An iron sword."

"It's Gosol – you have to know how to use it. Look, there's no time for explanations now. We must go after Briannan."

He signalled to the leader of the first boat and the sound of chanting began again. The boats began to glide over the ground as before, and Cosmo waved to everyone to run alongside. Oobit and the others arrived at the cave, and collapsed, exhausted.

"I need a rest," gasped Radge. "Who says exercise is good for you?"

"You'll have plenty of time to rest dead if the Brashat get you," replied Cosmo curtly.

He turned and started jogging after the boats, which had already got some twenty yards in front.

"Can't we get a lift in the boats?" asked Petros. Cosmo didn't turn round or speak. "Didn't think so," muttered the youngster.

Henri stepped up to Rana and knelt down. Then, pressing his right palm against her injured shoulder and his left hand behind her back, he squeezed. The shoulder throbbed for a few moments, then the pain eased. She smiled at the Frenchman, who nodded curtly and stood up.

Jack found the running easier than expected. Despite the terror he had felt when seized by Konan, Jack's face now flushed with excitement. Within minutes, he and Petros had reached the hermit's cell, but it was deserted. The boats were still ahead of them. They followed the sound of chanting.

Petros and Jack were soon overtaken by the Claville and Cos-Howe boys, but the Congress members – none of them

219

in the first flush of youth – were trailing. Grandpa, still limping badly, brought up the rear with the Darrig, who puffed and panted as he tried to keep up.

The Cos-Howe crew took a few minutes to reach the boats, which had halted as the forest thinned out. The chanting had stopped, and the bell in each boat was silent. Cosmo, marshalling his friends, explained what they must do. About a hundred yards away, across a clearing, was the ruined castle. A ramshackle affair, it looked ready to tumble down at any minute. Torches blazed from ruined windows, and the sound of raucous festivities carried across the clearing. Jack collapsed happily on the ground.

"What's the plan, then?" he asked, his face beaming with expectation.

Despite it being a clear crisp night, his palms were sweaty, and his heart raced. Petros, Rana and Lizzie arrived, falling in a heap.

"This isn't a game, you know," said Cosmo heatedly. "We couldn't afford to leave you at the cave – there might be stray Brashat around. But this is about to get really serious. We'll have to attack the castle. We need the Congress members, but you kids will have to sit this one out."

"What d'you mean?" exclaimed Jack. "We've done all right so far. If I hadn't escaped and fetched you, and called the monks, the Congress would still be prisoners."

"Jack, I fetched *you* from behind that rock," said Cosmo quietly. "And the boats are our trump card. The Brashat won't be able to handle them. But it's dangerous. They're vicious. One of them already tried to kill you."

"But I got the better of him with the Aximon."

"Jack," Cosmo took him firmly by the shoulder, "you've not been trained for this. You're not armed. This isn't like kids fighting, don't you understand?"

"If you let us use sceptres we'd be OK," mumbled Jack.

"Jack, you know you're not old enough to use a sceptre."

"I'm nearly old enough," declared Petros.

"Not until you're fourteen," pointed out Cosmo. "But Ossian can use one."

"I'm better off wi' a club," said Ossian. "The others can stick wi' me."

At that moment the Congress members arrived, all of them panting heavily. Jack saw that Armina had joined them. As if to greet their arrival, a volley of arrows flew past, whistling into the trees behind. Jeering laughter and insults came from the castle.

"Get down!" ordered Cosmo, but the Congress members needed no encouragement. A second volley of arrows flew overhead, hitting no one, but accompanied, as before, by a torrent of abuse.

"The Brashat never were any good at that," smirked Radge. "Let's get at them."

"We'll let the boats go in first," said Cosmo. "That'll confuse them. If they feel the iron coming, they may even run. But we have to get the Chalice. Henri, can you get behind the castle to stop them escaping? Take your boys and Radge and Tom, and one of the boats."

The leader of the second boat seemed to understand, for immediately it turned and skirted around the castle, taking a wide arc. Henri and the others ran alongside.

While they got into position, Cosmo outlined his plan of attack to a stern-faced Atholmor. Unused to being outranked, especially by someone so much younger than him, the Congress leader could only acknowledge Cosmo's authority at this time. Cosmo then turned and spoke quietly to Doonya. Doonya called his daughters over and put his arm protectively around them both.

Jack and Petros sat and watched the castle, eerily silent now; all the torches had been extinguished. Jack was wondering how on earth they would get the Brashat out and the Chalice back, when the chanting began again, louder than ever.

Gosol! Gosol! Gosol!

Then, clearly visible in the bright moonlight, the Brashat began to emerge. Thirty or forty of them, headed by Briannan, each wore a long dark green cloak. Forming a phalanx, they advanced, their outstretched hands free of weapons. Two old hags in black cloaks flew around at the rear, swooping and turning, cackling shrilly. Jack could see Hobshee scurrying around at the back. While some clung nervously to the coat-tails of the Brashat, others peeked fearfully from windows and doorways.

Briannan held the Cup high above his head as he walked proudly forward. Brightly polished now, it shone brilliantly. Rowan walked self-assuredly just behind him.

The phalanx got to about twenty yards away and stopped.

"This is the night of Hallows' Eve, when all the witchies ride!" chanted Briannan triumphantly.

The chanting from the boats diminished slightly, but Cosmo stepped forward and shouted back, "*This is the night of Hallows' Eve, the morn is Hallows' Day!*"

Briannan paused, his face showing the first signs of doubt.

"Tonight is the night for all Shian," he proclaimed. "And tonight the Unseelie have the prize sought by so many for so long." He brandished the Cup again.

"You're a thief!" shouted Atholmor.

A thief's brief reward, thought Jack. *Tamlina said that.*

"But we have the Cup," Briannan shouted back. "The power over death – even over Nature! You think your boats of ghosts can take it from us? The memories of holy men? Then Hallows' Eve or no, prepare to die."

Each Brashat now drew out a sceptre. The Hobshee, gaining confidence, brandished their clubs, howling in excitement. But as the phalanx moved forward, a different sound came from the forest behind Jack, a sound of drumming. No, not drumming, but something rhythmic and harsh, getting louder and louder. The Brashat halted, not ten yards from the boats, and the Hobshee began whimpering again. Everyone turned to look at the forest.

Then Jack saw them. Three mighty longships, a dragon's head at the prow of each, gliding through the forest. They dwarfed the other boats, and Jack could see the warriors lining the sides of these mighty ships.

Did I summon them too?!

Brandishing axes and swords, the warriors beat these noisily against round wooden shields. Some of the Brashat started to back away.

"Face them! Face them!" bellowed Briannan, sensing the unease in his ranks. "They're only ghosts!"

Then Grandpa Sandy stepped out and confronted Briannan.

"Only ghosts?" he roared, overcoming his pain. "*This is the night of Hallows' Eve, when more than ghosties ride!*"

Briannan, looking behind Grandpa, staggered back, still clutching the Cup. His face showed abject terror.

The next moment, the longships broke through the edge of the forest.

32
The Hidden Commonwealth

It wasn't really a battle. As the longships crashed through the edge of the forest, the Brashat broke ranks and scattered. Leaping from the boats, warriors laid into the terrified Brashat and Hobshee, their swords and axes making mayhem. Jack saw several fall, hacked and bleeding. Briannan vainly ordered his followers to stand their ground, but it was already too late. In a matter of seconds, a longship had out-paced those who tried to head back to the castle. Behind it, Henri, Tom and Radge hexed the Brashat that were left there as they ran in terror. The two flying hags made off into the night, screaming obscenities.

Rowan and several Brashat ran panic-stricken for the cover of the trees, but Cosmo urged the others on to prevent them. Sceptres were levelled at the fleeing figures, and bolt after bolt lit up the gloom of the forest's edge. Those who had been hit lay, alive but motionless.

Ossian and the Darrig stood by the edge of the trees. As those Brashat who had escaped the sceptre bolts came within range, they swung their clubs. Jack and Petros picked up branches from the ground and joined in. They each sheltered behind a tree and tripped up and knocked unconscious the panicked Brashat and Hobshee as they sought safety. Surreptitiously, Jack snatched one of the Brashat's sceptres and concealed it inside his coat. Further back in the woods, Doonya stood shielding Rana and Lizzie, who tried desperately to see what was happening.

Grandpa and Atholmor advanced towards Briannan, a lonely general deserted by his troops. Longships flanked him to left and right. Those warriors who had not already descended now did so, and they advanced menacingly, their axes gleaming. Briannan looked desperately around, seeking an avenue of escape, but his group was surrounded.

"I'll destroy the Cup!" he shouted in a desperate bid to assert his authority. Holding it aloft with his left hand, he pointed his sceptre at it.

Without warning, a fiery glow erupted on the roof of the ruined castle, and there was a rumble of thunder. Jack could see a figure in the red glow, tall and powerful looking, and with a single horn on his right side of his forehead. The figure swayed backwards and forwards, and then Jack saw that several smaller creatures were restraining it. A loud hissing noise came from its mouth, like a fire over which water has been thrown. With a loud thunder crack, the air turned ice cold, and Jack felt a wave of fear run through him.

"It's Amadan!" shrieked Armina.

Briannan and the remaining Brashat now started to make a fight of it. They fired volleys of hexes at the approaching warriors, some of whom fell, soundlessly. Jack saw Radge, emerging from behind the castle, catching the full force of a lightning hex and crumpling instantly.

On the roof, Amadan seemed to grow even taller. Sparks flew from his hands, and a longship mast burst into flames, fiery splinters cascading over the warriors below. Atholmor, a look of terror on his face, leapt aside as a flaming timber crashed to the ground beside him.

"Rally! Rally!" called Briannan exultantly, and Jack could see the Brashat warriors growing in confidence as Amadan's hexes found their mark.

The tide had turned. Cosmo and the Congress members were sheltering beneath the meagre protection of a fallen tree. The Norse warriors were being decimated, and several monks lay lifeless. Then, with horror, Jack saw Amadan point his right forefinger at Grandpa Sandy.

"No!" Jack leapt forward, his blue eye ablaze. He withdrew the sceptre he had hidden inside his own coat – but it was too late. A bolt flew from Amadan's hand, there was a loud snapping sound, and Grandpa fell, immobile.

No! This wasn't supposed to happen!

Crouching to shield his grandfather's body, Jack raised his sceptre, and aimed it at the rooftop figure.

"Gosol!"

A lightning bolt shot forward, sparkling as it flew, and the rooftop figure staggered. Seeing this, Cosmo raised his own sceptre.

"Gosol!"

The double bolts crackled as they flew towards the roof. It felt like a ton weight was pushing his arm down, but Jack kept his sceptre steady. Amadan rocked backwards and forwards, and stumbled, at which a great shout came from the monks.

"*Gosol! Gosol! Gosol!*"

Amadan gave an ear-splitting roar as he was subsumed into a huge sheet of flame. The inferno rose up from the roof and spiralled into a great dart, which veered first upwards, then down towards where Jack crouched over his grandfather's body. The fiery dart bore down on the youngster, scattering all before it.

Jack's arm ached, and he felt it falling as the dart approached. Gritting his teeth, he forced himself to keep his sceptre up. At the last second, Amadan swerved upwards, passing over Jack's head and burning the side of his face. The fire faded into a glow in the air above Jack, then disappeared with a final *crack*! The Brashat warriors, their inspiration snatched away, deflated like a stabbed balloon. Exhausted, Jack sank down.

Complete silence.

Jack shook his head, and looked round at his grandfather.

He's not breathing!

In a panic, Jack shouted across to Briannan, "Give me the Cup! It can save Grandpa!"

And then the bell chimed.

A single bell, it tolled steadily in the still air, even, unhurried.

Twelve chimes.

An eerie silence descended. Even the dying Brashat stopped their moaning.

"*Hallows' Eve is past, is past, and now 'tis Hallows' Day!*"

The first boat's lead figure had broken his silence, his voice clear and strong. Stepping down from the boat, he advanced towards Briannan. Floating as his colleague had done at the cave, the figure passed through the warriors and stopped in front of the Brashat leader. Even in the moonlight, Jack could see Briannan's face turn yet paler as he looked around at his defeated comrades. His arms sagged. Cup and sceptre dropped to the ground. Sinking to his knees, he summoned his last reserves of defiance and shouted, "Then kill me!"

The monk stood, impassive. Then he put his right hand into his cloak. Briannan waited for the sword to be drawn, but instead the figure drew out a small phial. He pulled a cloth plug from its neck, and poured a little oil onto Briannan's head. Collapsing back, Briannan lay motionless. The monk then stooped down and picked up the Cup. A cheer rose from the boats, then the chant rose again, urgently calling, "*Gosol! Gosol! Gosol!*"

The monk glided over to where Jack sat, hunched over his grandfather. Looking down into the boy's tear-stained face, he smiled and handed him the Cup, then reached into his cloak and withdrew a ram's horn. He pulled out the stopper and poured some red liquid into the Cup.

Cradling his grandfather's head, Jack tipped some of the fluid into his mouth. Most of it spilled down, but some dribbled in. Jack waited expectantly.

But nothing happened.

Jack wiped some of the spilled liquid from his grandfather's face.

Nothing.

"I thought it was supposed to defeat death!" Jack shouted at the monk, looking up imploringly. The monk remained standing there, impassive.

"If you believe."

"He *should* live. He *deserves* to. And we need him. *Please*."

Hot tears ran down Jack's cheeks now, and he glared angrily at the monk, who merely smiled back, and nodded down at Grandpa Sandy.

"He's not dead."

Following his gaze, Jack saw his grandfather's eyelids flicker. Then a gasping noise, and Grandpa Sandy shook slightly before pushing himself into a sitting position.

"Did I . . . bring him back?" Jack looked up at the monk.

"You believed."

"*Gosol! Gosol! Gosol!*"

The warriors joined in now, clashing their swords and axes once more against their shields. The noise built to a deafening crescendo, then the figure held up his hand, and there was silence.

The monk took the Cup back from Jack and glided back to where Briannan lay motionless. Picking up the Brashat's sceptre, he shot a bolt into the sky, which began to glow, softly at first, then more brightly. The clearing, bathed in moonlight up to now, looked almost as if it was in daylight. As the light rose, the bodies of the slain ghosts seemed to evaporate, and a rumbling sound came from the earth. Over the next minute, a stepped forum began to sink into the ground.

And suddenly the sky was filled with creatures. Not since midsummer had Jack seen so many different kinds. Horses and pisgies landed, depositing their riders in the clearing. Phooka cantered in from the edge of the forest, Elle-folk and korrigans skipped past the trees to join the throng.

Tomte and Nisse, the Congress dwarves, appeared beside Atholmor, just as Samara arrived with Henri's brother Philippe; and there was Matthew, the referee from Claville, still clutching his leather-bound volume. And Murkle, standing alone, but smiling, clearly in his element.

"Where've they all come from?" asked Petros, of no one in particular.

Jack shrugged his shoulders. Tonight had almost lost its power to amaze him. Rana, Lizzie and Doonya approached.

"Are you all all right?" asked Doonya anxiously.

"We're fine," beamed Petros. "That was awesome, though, eh?"

"We weren't allowed to join in," pouted Rana.

"It wasn't a game," said her father in exasperation. "You'd already been attacked once."

"It just sort of grazed me," said Rana confidently. "And Henri fixed it. My shoulder's grand."

"Jack, you'd better let Armina see that burn on your face."

As Jack went over to find Armina, Petros asked, "So what's happening now, then?"

As if in answer, the ghost monk held aloft the Cup, and once more there was silence.

"I am Comgall," he announced, his voice clear and strong. "We were summoned this night to rescue the Chalice from those who would follow evil. Many will claim the Chalice tonight. There has been bloodshed, but we come to proclaim not warfare but peace."

Doonya ushered the youngsters towards their grandfather – looking ashen – and the other Congress members. Henri, Philippe and Matthew joined them with Ossian and the Cos-Howe crew. Jack walked up, holding a small stone to his burnt face.

To their left were the few remaining longship warriors. Across from them, the ghost monks. A small space around these groups betrayed the Shian fear of their iron axes and swords. Fenrig and Morrigan were made to sit beside the hexed Brashat, who, along with Briannan, had been laid out on the steps. The Phooka, Elle-folk and other Shian found seats where they could.

There was an expectant hush. Comgall and Matthew walked down to the base of the forum. Comgall cradled the Chalice carefully, as if it were a newborn baby. Matthew addressed the whole congregation.

"The King's Chalice has been found after many years. Shian, you are all part of the great hidden commonwealth – what the human world rarely sees or knows. You are summoned to partake in an historic decision. While for some tonight is their journey's end," he gestured towards the dead Brashat and Hobshee, "the lives of many have been spared."

He looked hard at those Brashat who were starting to come round from their hexes.

"The old ways have gone. The Shian world cannot return to the past. More and more, you must live alongside the humans. For some," and now Matthew looked over at Petros, Rana and Lizzie, "they are even your cousins."

"The Dameves have pushed us to the very edge of our

world!" Rowan had now recovered enough to shout. "Would you let them push us over?"

Oobit levelled his sceptre at Rowan, which had the effect of shutting him up.

"All creatures are connected – in heaven and on earth and under the earth. The hidden commonwealth must now decide the destiny of the Chalice."

33
The Destiny of the Chalice

"The Chalice does not grant power over death, as some have claimed," announced Matthew. "Nor does it control Nature – that is *infama*. But on exceptional days, a true believer's love can win out, even up to the point of death. It was made for Comgall and his monks, who taught that death is not the end. Summoned tonight, they are more than human ghosts, for ghosts cannot wield swords."

"Their swords are iron." Another Brashat spoke up. "Even dead, the humans are a danger to Shian."

"Yes, our swords are iron, like the axes of the longship warriors," said Comgall.

A large warrior stood up, and Jack sensed some of the crowd shrinking back as he brandished his axe.

"These Norse warriors plundered Comgall's abbey," interjected Matthew. "That is why they came tonight; they are linked with this place. In life, some went on to Ireland, leaving the Chalice there. Many years after, it turned up in the French king's court. Centuries later, it was gifted to a prince who came to these lands, but the prince lost it in a wager with a chieftain, who followed him to war. A love rival killed the chieftain's son, and hid the Chalice in a cave. Legends grew around it. In time, these were written down. Finding that book laid bare the location of the Chalice."

The Brashat, slowly recovering from their hexes, muttered amongst themselves, but none dared to speak.

"So who's going to get it, then?" asked Jack. "This is getting complicated."

Petros shrugged his shoulders.

"My friends," began Cosmo, stepping forward, "the Stone's return did not bring the prosperity we expected. But it is only one of three treasures; the Chalice is another. The third – an ancient globe – remains lost. Manuscripts tell of three treasures producing a great power. The Stone and the Chalice should be together. In time, we hope the globe will join them."

Briannan got unsteadily to his feet. "We do not have the Stone. The Dameves have it, with iron rings in a glass-iron case we cannot break. Would you give them the Cup as well?"

Grandpa Sandy got up now. His voice was weak again, and he swayed alarmingly. "It is true that iron prevents us from touching the Stone, but there is no doubt that it gives us much of our old power. And if the Chalice helps, then it *must* go to the Stone, in the humans' castle."

"That means that only you can see them!" retorted Briannan, his strength returning.

"If the Chalice goes to one group, I fear there will be warfare for years," said Matthew. "In and below the humans' castle it can be shared by all – Shian and human. The triple spiral represents something above both human and Shian worlds."

"Then what does it mean?" demanded Briannan.

"To answer that we must find the Sphere," said Cosmo. "But the treasures are linked. The Chalice must be shared between the Shian square and the Stone Room in the humans' castle."

Briannan was not persuaded, but the close attention of the Cos-Howe contingent, who kept their sceptres trained on the remnants of his army, prevented him from making any moves. There was a general murmuring around the forum as the various groups discussed what should happen. Gradually the muttering softened, and one of the Elle-folk stood up.

"We have links to the Norse ghosts. The Chalice did not bring them success for long. We agree that it can join the Stone, as long as they belong to all Shian."

Jack, his burnt face now almost healed, saw Atholmor and Grandpa Sandy – apparently recovered – whispering urgently. Then Atholmor stood up.

"We concede that the treasures must be shared. We will arrange for the Chalice to be kept in the humans' castle and in the Shian square, six months each."

"Thank you," said Matthew. "And do the Phooka and the pisgies also agree?"

There was a brief flurry of excitement within each group, and then the answer came back that yes, they had reached the same conclusion. The korrigan and the dwarves also indicated their assent, but Tomte, the Congress dwarf, stood up, glowering.

"But what will happen to the Brashat? They stole the Chalice for their own ends. They will threaten us again if they are not taken care of."

"The Brashat who took part in tonight's battle will be punished," said Matthew. "But the world has changed. Although our Norse friends do not agree, the punishment is no longer death."

"Put them to the iron!" shouted Henri. "It is the punishment for all Unseelie who cause mayhem."

Jack recalled how Grulsh's friends had been melted into the war memorial in Claville. Some of the Brashat had obviously heard of this punishment too, for they started twitching nervously.

"We will not be putting them to the iron," said Cosmo firmly.

"And have them return to kill us in our beds?" shouted Tomte.

"They will be punished, but a just punishment, to be decided here by the whole commonwealth. Three years suspended is fair."

"Five years!" shouted a voice from the assembly.

Jack stood up. "My father's suspended ten years, and I don't even know where he is!"

There was a moment of silence. Grandpa put his hand gently on Jack's shoulder. Jack didn't know what he felt. While delighted that they had retrieved the Chalice, still his anger cried out for the Brashat to be punished.

A sneering look came over Briannan's face.

"Konan escaped, but your fool of a father didn't. He'll be there forever."

"I hope you rot there forever!" shouted Jack angrily, tears in his eyes. "And if Konan's so smart, how come he's dead?"

"Jack," said his grandfather softly, "Konan's not dead. And Briannan will be punished. Being suspended is like feeling you'll never get away. It empties you." Then he saw Jack's sad eyes reproaching him.

"I'm sorry. That makes it no easier for you. But we have to remember that tonight Briannan has been defeated. We must not be bitter in our victory."

Cosmo came up. "He's right, Jack. It's difficult, but the power of Gosol demands that we are not vengeful."

"If Gosol's so powerful, how come it can't bring my parents back to me?" shouted Jack, fighting back the tears.

"I . . . I don't know." Cosmo tried to smile reassuringly, but Jack's pain wouldn't go away.

Cosmo then turned and indicated to Comgall and the Cos-Howe crew. The Brashat and Hobshee were made to stand together, Briannan and Rowan at the front.

"For your part in the theft of this Chalice, which belongs to all, and for your collective attempts to kill several children, you will be put in suspension for a period of three years," said Atholmor sternly. "You will be kept in the Cave of the Skulls. Your own children will be spared; their part can be excused."

Without further word, Atholmor pointed his sceptre at the group, and a bolt shot from it. The Brashat and Hobshee began to glow, then rose from the ground as one. Then, over just a few seconds, they faded from view.

Jack saw Morrigan hug Fenrig, under the watchful eyes of Oobit and Tom. For a few moments, there was silence around the forum. Comgall pointed Briannan's sceptre upwards once more, and slowly the night sky began to darken. Even with the moonlight, it took Jack's eyes some time to readjust.

"The Fool of the Forth has terrorised a weak and divided Shian for centuries. But he is no match for those who truly believe in the power of goodness, and who have the Chalice," announced Matthew. "You must work now to discover the Sphere, to complete the trinity of treasures. Go well. Go in peace."

"Time to go," said Doonya simply, ushering the youngsters together. "We'll use the low road, that's quickest. It's the hermit's cell. Ossian can fly the horses back to Keldy."

"You mean we could've used a low road to get here?" asked Rana.

"It's just as well we didn't know about it, though," replied Jack. "If we had, we wouldn't have asked Ossian to help, then we wouldn't have had Cosmo and the others."

"Who was that up on the castle roof, Dad?" asked Petros.

"That was Amadan – the Fool of the Forth. His demons were pulling him back – they must have sensed the power we had with the Chalice. He doesn't often beat a retreat, but we got the better of him somehow."

"You mean, Jack took on Amadan?" said Petros breathlessly. "Wicked!"

"Jack weakened him, and Cosmo helped to finish him off," continued Doonya. "That was brave of you, Jack, but you know you're not supposed to use a sceptre."

Jack felt drained. Praised and scolded in the one sentence. Wordlessly, he handed the sceptre over to his uncle. There was so much he didn't understand, but he could take no more in just now. Lizzie yawned, and it was infectious.

"Time to get you lot home," said Doonya gently. "Armina will take Grandpa back."

"What'll happen to Fenrig?" asked Jack. "Will he go back to his mother?"

"It's a long story, Jack, but Fenrig's mother's not around. I think Atholmor would rather have him and his sister where he can keep an eye on them. That's why Atholmor allowed Fenrig under the castle in the first place. He knows Fenrig's not the brightest candle in the box; he hoped that he'd give away more than he found out."

"You mean, they won't be punished at all?" said Petros.

"They're young, and they were led by their father. They can't be blamed for what he did. But you lot will have to keep an eye on them for us."

"Fenrig's not that stupid," said Jack, a thousand thoughts whirling around in his mind. "He worked out how to make himself invisible; he stole the manuscripts, and found out about us going for the Cup."

"You're right. We underestimated him. We won't make that mistake again."

Once all were inside what was left of the hermit's cell, Doonya put his cloak around the four youngsters.

"Wind-flock castle!" he called, and Jack felt the by now familiar spinning sensation.

It was the longest low road journey Jack had made, although it still only took a few minutes. Jack's head buzzed with thoughts, but he was too tired to make sense of these now. He just wanted to fall into bed.

34
The Reluctant Hero

Jack slept like a log, but when he finally awoke, he still felt drained. The Chalice was safe, and the Brashat beaten, but somehow he felt hollow. He found Rana and Lizzie in the kitchen, whispering together, and giggling. *Why do girls do that?* he wondered.

Aunt Katie came in, and beamed a sad smile at him. "You've no idea what you put me through, disappearing like that."

"We were fine, Mum," said Lizzie as she cradled a restless Nuxie. "We can look after ourselves."

"Aye, well, I'm just glad to get you all back in one piece."

"Have I missed work today?"

"It doesn't matter. Grandpa's explained things to Gilmore. He says you can have tomorrow morning off as well, but you'll have your lesson with Daid after lunch."

"Is Grandpa OK?" asked Jack.

"Armina's checked him over – she says he's grand," said Aunt Katie happily. "And did she look at that burn on your face?"

"It's fine; she put some cold charm stones on it. She says there won't be a scar."

"There'll be a big party in the square on Friday evening."

"We're celebrating getting the Cup," announced Rana.

"The Chalice, you mean," said Katie. "We'll have to learn to call it that. The Congress are arranging for it to be placed in the castle. The humans will be delighted – they love all that historical stuff."

"So we really do have to give it to them, then?"

"Share it – it will move between the human space up above and here. We have common concerns. It's just taken some Shian longer to realise that, that's all. Our family – well, you know our history."

"Realise what?" asked Petros, entering the room and yawning expansively.

"That things are changing," said his mother. "Now, what would you all like to eat?"

After lunch the next day, Jack made his way to Daid's house. He could see the other apprentices whispering amongst themselves as he approached.

"Hi, Jack," called out Purdy. "We heard you had some fun yesterday. Are you going to tell us about it?"

"Was your granddad really dead? And you charmed him back?" Kaol's eyes were wide with admiration.

"No, I—"

"Did you really meet ghost warriors?" gasped Séan. "What happened when the Brashat got suspended?"

"And you even attacked Amadan?" Boyce gave Jack a look that might almost have been respect. "The baddest Unseelie of the lot? I heard he can kill just by looking at you."

The questions bewildered Jack – there was still so much to piece together in his own mind. Relief flooded through him as Daid opened the front door and ushered the class in.

When they were all seated, Daid began.

"I'm sure we'd all like to hear Jack's stories about Dunvik, but we need to give him some space, so I propose to tell you a little of the Cup's background."

There was an audible sigh of disappointment around the room, but the apprentices settled down to listen.

"The tales are in Purdy's book. Around a hundred and fifty years ago, a rather eccentric woman went travelling around the more remote parts of the country. She later published her journal of stories. One was the legend of a chalice, plundered by Vikings and returned centuries later by a young prince, come to fight for the throne. He was a very *human* human, if you know what I mean, having a fondness for gambling and strong drink."

Séan and Boyce exchanged knowing smirks.

"Well, he gambled away the Cup, and it got passed to a chieftain's son, who loved a beautiful young woman. But she was betrothed to a poor fisherman, and when the two men quarrelled, the chieftain's son was killed. The fisherman panicked and hid in a cave. Sadly for him, the cave was a 'thin place', an entrance to the Shian world, and the creatures under the cave lured him away from the Cup and killed him. But the fisherman must have charmed the Cup, because the Shian couldn't move it. Once a year, the Cup would glow on Hallows' Eve."

"I heard Briannan got the Cup," interjected Boyce.

"But he couldn't keep it, could he?" replied Daid. "And he could only take it because he found it on Hallows' Eve. The charm must not work then. Now, I'm afraid that I have stolen some of young Purdy's storyline. Purdy, is there anything you'd like to add?"

Relieved not to be the focus of attention, Jack settled back while Purdy spoke about the rest of the book. His thoughts drifted off to what Briannan had said.

Your fool of a father.

Why hadn't his father been able to escape, like Konan had? There were so many things he didn't understand.

Jack left quickly at the end of the lesson, but when he went home his aunt informed him that the Congress was making arrangements for the Chalice to be deposited in the castle. Jack would have to wait until that evening to speak to his grandfather.

Evening came and went with no sign of Grandpa. When Jack asked his uncle, he got a non-committal reply. His uncle seemed distant, his mind on other things. Aunt Katie explained that Doonya had been concerned about Rana and Lizzie.

Aunt Katie doesn't change much, thought Jack. Always trying to smooth things over, but always anxious. And the girls, to judge by their actions since returning, had been most concerned about Nuxie.

Work the next day felt strange. Freya was keen to get his news, but Gilmore kept them hard at it, insisting that they complete their tasks before the weekend. Jack wondered if all teachers were as irritating as this. Doxer, as quiet as ever, worked away patiently and silently. Fenrig, Freya explained (having heard this from her father), was being kept away until things settled down.

Over lunch, Freya quizzed Jack about Dunvik. Did the shifter work properly? How had Petros felt about the beetler? Was it safe to shrink down to that size out in the open? Jack tried to answer Freya's questions, but inside there was a whirling mix of his own. Relieved when the working day was over, he made his way wearily back to the house.

"You'll never guess who's playing at the party!" announced Rana breathlessly as he entered the house.

"It's the Sceptres!" gasped Lizzie, before Rana could draw out the suspense. "And Glownie's coming too."

"The Sceptres are the best musicians in the country," Petros explained to Jack, who was looking nonplussed. "They're from the islands; they don't visit the cities much."

"Uncle Hart's coming too. He might play along with Glownie," said Rana. "I can't wait."

"The Cos-Howe lot will definitely come when they hear who's playing," said Lizzie excitedly.

Jack was still trying to make sense of Dunvik, but his younger cousins had just accepted things.

Maybe it's easier that way. Maybe I'm thinking too much about it all.

Predictably, when the adults started to arrive, everyone was too busy talking to talk to him. Grandpa Sandy (fully recovered, it seemed) and Atholmor were deep in conversation with Festus and Murkle, and Jack didn't feel like interrupting them. He certainly didn't feel up to tackling Murkle. Jack listened while Lizzie recounted to Freya how the invisible bonnets had been great fun, and could they have a spare set, please? They were so fine and light that she could see a time when they would need to be repaired.

The crowd and the noise grew. Jack had never seen the square so full, and indeed there had not been that many Shian there for many years. People were happy; there was a tangible sense of relief. But Jack didn't feel like joining in, and this irritated him. It wasn't just tiredness, or the adrenaline come-down – the others had got over all that. This was something else.

As the musicians got ready on the stage, Jack found himself wandering to the side wall. Almost absent-mindedly, he placed his left hand on the rock wall and whispered, "*Effatha!*"

35
Reasons To Be Cheerful

Jack was half-surprised when, moments later, he found himself in the dark by the castle chapel. He wandered around to the deserted rampart walls over which he'd first seen the city spread before him. Midsummer was a world away. Jack shivered as he gazed at the glowing lights of the New Town far below.

All those humans, and now we're told our destinies are shared. How can we be Shian if we have to mix with them? Something must get lost.

Jack leant against the wall, his chin on his forearms, and pondered.

A cough startled him out of his reverie. Wheeling round, his first impulse was to run, but a reassuring voice said, "Don't worry, Jack. It's just me."

With a surge of relief, he recognised his grandfather's voice.

"I got a fright." His heart was still pounding.

"Don't you fancy coming to the party?"

"I just wanted a bit of space. I can't get my head around everything, you know, up in Dunvik."

"I know. And I'm sorry I haven't been around to answer your questions since we got back. We had to make arrangements about the Chalice, but that's done now. But first of all I must thank you for stepping in when I got hurt. Your exceptional courage tipped the balance. Amadan couldn't cope with what you did. We're all in your debt."

"I thought he'd killed you."

"He had. But somewhere inside, you found the strength – and the belief – to challenge that. And you could never have done it without the Chalice. You *believed* in it, Jack."

"I just knew it was the right thing to do. Gosol's not just a charm, is it?"

His grandfather looked across at him kindly. "Gosol's about everything being joined up. Like everything you do having an effect on everyone else. And it's doing the right thing for the right reason. You must have really believed it for it to work – like when Konan had you by the throat. You kept your head and used the Aximon, didn't you? It could only work if you truly believed. Gosol and the Aximon know this."

"Tamlina was right," said Jack quietly. "I *had* met Konan before. He tried to grab me on the High Street at midsummer, but I got away."

"Jack," said his grandfather after a few moments, "you should have told us. We don't want to keep you in a cage, but we can't expose you to risks like that."

"So what did happen to Konan?"

"I know you thought your uncle had killed him, but

Doonya fused him into that oak. It's a hex – Konan's alive, just part of the tree. I doubt he'll ever get away."

"So he's as good as dead, then?"

"In the past there would have been no question. Attacking Shian children would have earned a death sentence. But you heard what was said: Gosol demands that we have more respect for life than that."

"But that monk killed the Brashat who attacked Rana," pointed out Jack.

"He thought she'd been killed. He was trying to prevent more deaths."

"If Konan's still alive, he might be able to tell us where my father is."

"You never know. A counter-hex might work. As for finding your father, well, we know more now than we knew a while ago. And it wasn't the Brashat who suspended him; that was the Grey. So, we can keep looking."

"What about my mother and Cleo?" Jack's voice was almost a whisper.

"The Brashat are out of the frame for a while. If she hears of it, your mother may feel it's safe to return."

"But after everything in Dunvik, we don't even get to keep the Chalice. We searched for it, and found it. Now we've got to share it with the humans – and even the Brashat."

"The whole point of the Chalice is not to own it, Jack, but to share it. And Matthew was right: if one group owned it, there'd be warfare."

"It's complicated," Jack said at last. "Some things you're sure of turn out to be lies. Like the Congress: Rowan was a traitor; he nearly got us killed."

Grandpa exhaled loudly. "Shian and humans are very alike in that respect. Some just want to be on the winning side. But if anything, he faces a worse punishment than the Brashat. He'll always be an outsider to them, and he knows we'll never trust him again."

Jack stared out across the rooftops of the city, the house and streetlights twinkling below. He found he could muster no sympathy for Rowan.

"There's other things I don't understand," he said eventually. "The Norse warriors and the monks were ghosts; they could hold iron axes and swords, so they're not Shian. How could they be part of a Shian battle?"

"There *were* ghosts. They appeared on Hallows' Eve because it's a special night, the kind of night when ghosts can be summoned. *You* did that with the ram's horn. That's why we could recover the Chalice too. It's called a 'thin time'; the boundaries between different worlds can be crossed. There's 'thin places' too, like the cave."

"But how come the ghosts didn't disappear at midnight? They were all chanting *Gosol,* and Comgall even spoke to the commonwealth."

"Over the centuries we managed to forget something. The clue is in the name. Christmas Eve doesn't mean much without Christmas Day, does it? The same goes for Hallows' Eve. We were only looking at the first half of things. A long time ago I must have been told this, because it came flooding back when Cosmo challenged Briannan. And it's like Matthew said: Briannan committed *infama* – a crime against Nature – when he thought the Chalice would give him power over death, and even Nature itself. The Chalice has Gosol, and Gosol is the *reason* for life; it's what's been there forever."

"The creator force?"

"Not just creation, but its *goodness*. That sureness gave me the strength to challenge Briannan. You saw the look on his face when the Norsemen came? Ghosts he could handle, because they would disappear at midnight, and they certainly would not have iron swords. '*More than ghosties*', well, Briannan couldn't handle that. And Hallows' Day is one of those exceptional days when the Chalice can show its power, as you proved."

"So the Chalice can defeat death, but only at certain times?"

"And only if you believe enough. It's not like a charm. Sadly, it didn't bring Radge back, though Tom tried."

For anyone to die is sad, thought Jack, but all the Cos-Howe crew came along knowing the risks. And we *did* get the Chalice, after all.

And yet something still gnawed away at Jack's insides.

"I feel I should be happier," he said dejectedly. "We beat the Brashat, and we got the Chalice, but I feel like something's missing."

"That's not hard to explain: we still haven't found your father. But you've a lot going for you. I know he doesn't always show it, but Doonya's really proud about what you did. It was your belief, a *real* belief in the rightness of what you were doing. That's the true power of Gosol, Jack. You used that when you attacked Amadan, and when you brought me back.

"Jack, you've done a lot of growing since you arrived from Rangie. This is not the end; there's the Sphere to seek now. We can't do much over the winter, but when spring returns we start again."

Jack smiled at the thought. Memories of carefree days in Rangie stirred in his mind.

"We'll start by looking for those manuscripts. Did you know it was Fenrig who left them in the chapel? He must have stolen them from his father. He's not letting on where they are, but we'll get them. And who knows? Maybe they'll lead us to your father. Now come on below to the party. It's cold, and the musicians will be playing soon."

Jack realised that it was indeed cold up on top of the castle. Things were beginning to make sense, slowly. As his grandfather put his arm around his shoulder, Jack felt a lot warmer inside. There *was* a lot that had gone well that week. And he did feel like hearing some music. They walked to the side of the chapel and were soon back in the Shian square.

Rana came running up. "Come on, Jack! The Sceptres are about to start!"

Even as she spoke, there was a crash of drums and a dramatic chord from guitar, fiddle and flute. Within seconds, the top of the square was a whirling reel of bodies and stamping feet.

Lizzie handed Jack a goblet of tayberry juice. "Cheers!"

Jack took the goblet and smiled back. It was good to be alive. He saw Cosmo and the other Cos-Howe boys in the throng, and Petros and Ossian talking with Purdy and Freya. Freya waved at him, urging him to join in as they threw themselves into the mass of dancing bodies.

There is more to do, thought Jack. But let's enjoy tonight.

Read on for a sneak peek of Book 2 in
The Shian Quest Trilogy . . .

JACK SHIAN
AND THE
MAPPA MUNDI

Coming Soon!

1

My Enemy's Enemy

The third echo was ... silence?

Silence preceded by a hollow emptiness.

Jack had just enough time to be surprised before his eardrums were hammered by a deafening thunderclap. Jumping in alarm, he clasped his hands over his ears.

Screaming, Lizzie tried to do the same – but too late. A trickle of blood emerged from her right ear, and she coorie into her grandfather.

Jack stared in disbelief as the Blue Hag swayed alarmingly on the small hill she had just climbed. Three times he had watched the old woman as she had shuffled up an incline to perform the ancient Shian ritual for clearing the snows at winter's end. Three times on reaching the top she had drawn her long staff upright and thudded it into the ground. Reverberations in the surrounding hills had melted the snow for fifty yards around her. Or at least they had done so twice. But the third time – nothing.

The staff had hit the ground, just like before. But this time, there was no sound – until the thunderclap. The Blue Hag steadied herself and peered round, perplexed. Her gaze passed over Jack, Lizzie and their grandfather, and came to rest on a much higher hill to Jack's left. He followed her eyes. There, standing at the very summit some two hundred yards away, he could just make out three figures. One of them waved something above his head – a sceptre perhaps? – and then came the sound of distant cheering. The sky above the figures darkened, there was a crack of thunder and a single lightning strike scorched a solitary tree on the hillside. Howling curses in their direction, the Blue Hag retreated quickly down the hillside.

"Who in Tua's name are they?" exclaimed Jack. The taste of treachery fouled his throat, like the time he'd realised Rowan had sold out the Congress four months earlier.

Grandpa Sandy had withdrawn his own sceptre from his cloak. Fingering it agitatedly, his stern look was fixed upon the distant figures. Jack saw him clench his jaw.

Lizzie rubbed her right ear and squeaked in alarm as she saw the blood. Cowering behind her grandfather's cloak, she peered fearfully at the distant figures as one of them rose from the ground and did a graceful pirouette in the air. The manoeuvre had lasted fully ten seconds. Grandpa's face relaxed, and he lowered his sceptre.

"Kildashie," he said simply, emphasising the second syllable. "I'd almost forgotten what they were like."

Jack looked again at the distant figures, but could make little out. Then he saw the one with the sceptre wave it in an arc above his head. There was another loud peal of thunder, and it began to rain. Not just ordinary raindrops: huge smudges of water that drenched within seconds.

"Why'd he do that?" complained Lizzie, trying to pull her coat over her head. "I'm all wet. And my ear hurts."

As more thunderclaps resounded around the hills, Grandpa Sandy waved at the figures, beckoning them over. After a short consultation, they began to glide from their hilltop, their cloaks flapping in the wind.

"Are they flying?" asked Jack. They reminded him of the two hags who had flown at the back of the Brashats at Dunvik.

"No, they can't fly." Grandpa kept his sceptre in his hand. "They live on islands far out into the ocean. They use their cloaks to glide."

The three men landed and made their way with effortless haste up towards them. Jack could see that they were all tall, with long straggly hair that swept about their faces. The one bearing the sceptre was in front, taking huge strides. Within seconds they had reached Jack and the others.

"Shian of Kildashie," said Grandpa Sandy slowly and evenly, "I have not seen you for many years. What brings you so far from your islands?"

Their leader stood, his long sceptre planted firmly on the ground. He gazed long and hard at Grandpa Sandy before replying.

"I am Tig, from Hilta. These are Boreus and Donar. We have come to renew old acquaintances, now the Brashat are vanquished."

"I well remember your dealings with the Brashat." Grandpa Sandy paused, considering how best to phrase things. "But you should know better than to interrupt the Blue Hag. She will be hard to placate now, and that will prolong our winter."

"What is that to us?" sneered Boreus. "Your sheltered winters are like Spring."

Jack squinted up at the rain-sodden sky. Dark clouds swept across the heavens, and the wind howled around them.

"But these are not your islands." Grandpa Sandy pressed his point home. "Here we mark the new Spring with this custom. You have disturbed the rhythm of the snow's end."

Boreus growled under his breath, and aimed his sceptre at a tree a little way down the slope. There was a flash, and the tree burst into flames. He moved forward menacingly, but was instantly halted by Tig's raised right forearm. Tig turned and muttered to his colleague, who retreated, scowling.

"I apologise if we have overstepped the bounds of hospitality," said Tig with an ingratiating smile. "We hope to be able to join you in the celebration of your Spring." He looked up at the sky, his brow furrowed briefly, then he waved his sceptre expansively over his head. The skies lightened appreciably. The rain dwindled to little more than a drizzle, and the wind dropped.

Lizzie, impressed, stepped out confidently from behind her grandfather. The ringing in her ears had stopped.

"How did you stop the echo?"

Tig looked sternly at her, and she quickly averted her gaze.

"My granddaughter is eager to learn," said Grandpa Sandy, putting his arm protectively around Lizzie's shoulder.

"There are times for lessons, and times to watch in wonder," said Tig evenly. "We will leave you now. But there is much we need to discuss with your Congress. Tell Atholmor that we wish to see him soon."

Without further word, the three Kildashie turned and strode off.

Jack had remained silent since their arrival. As the Kildashie reached the edge of the wood he turned to his grandfather.

"Grandpa, I don't trust them. Stopping the Blue Hag's *infama*, isn't it?"

"*Infama*? You mean against Nature?" asked Lizzie.

"You may be right, Jack," said Grandpa. "They're wild, I'll grant you that."

"I got the same feeling as I got with Konan last year." Jack thought back to his first encounter with Konan the Brashat in Edinburgh's High Street, and their subsequent clash at Dunvik just before the battle.

"They *are* rather uncivilised," his grandfather conceded. "I'd heard rumours that they've destroyed a lot of trees on their islands, and they don't seem to mind being out in the winter weather, like we do."

"Then they could attack us in the winter time, when we're all sheltering."

"Well, that's possible, but I think we can manage them. There's only a handful of them. They're also sworn enemies of the Brashat, so you've something in common there."

"Our enemy's enemy?" asked Lizzie.

"How come you've never mentioned them before?" demanded Jack. "And where are these islands?"

"Let's find the Blue Hag first, shall we?" said his grandfather. "We should see if we can't get her on the hills again."

"She went down that way," said Lizzie. "D'you think she'll come back?"

Grandpa led the two youngsters down the hill, but away from the woods into which the Kildashie had vanished. A few minutes later they came upon the Blue Hag. Wrapped in her cloak, she was huddled down, muttering to herself, and fingering a small wooden wheel. Grandpa held up his hand to stop Jack and Lizzie. Slowly he edged forward.

"*Cailleach*," he began, at which she raised her head. "We have seen your power in putting the snows of winter to flight. The Kildashie lack the understanding of your ways, but they have left. Will you continue now?"

The old woman looked at Grandpa Sandy for a moment, then snorted derisively and turned her face away. Grandpa Sandy returned to Jack and Lizzie and ushered them quickly away.

"We can stay in the bothy tonight. By tomorrow she may have forgotten the Kildashie."

He led the youngsters along the edge of the trees to a small wooden hut.

"Grandpa, d'you really trust the Kildashie?" asked Jack as Grandpa kindled a fire. "I got a bad feeling about them."

"I want to know how they stopped the echo," said Lizzie.

"It must be to do with the wind," said Grandpa. "They live with it."

"I got a funny feeling, like I was empty inside."

"It made my ear bleed," moaned Lizzie.

"The Kildashie *are* strange; their islands are far out into the western ocean. Living in such a bleak place has made them . . . shall we say, uncivilised? By reputation, all they fear is another Norse invasion."

"You mean like at Dunvik last year?"

"That's right, Lizzie. And you saw how fierce those warriors could be. But they only came because of the Chalice."

"Do the Kildashie mix with the humans, Grandpa?" queried Jack.

"The humans left the islands many years ago. The living got too tough for them – or maybe the Kildashie did. The Kildashie were forced onto the islands by the Brashat. There's no love lost between them."

Jack thought that he ought to feel more kindly towards the Kildashie, but he didn't.

"There's something about them I didn't trust. Controlling sound could be dangerous. And interrupting the Blue Hag, that's wrong, isn't it?"

"What they did was quite impressive. But you're right: breaking the Spring rite was *infama*. They should have had more respect."

Jack scowled. The way Boreus had moved towards him had definitely been threatening. Grandpa, however, would hear no more about it, and instead turned to the stories about the Blue Hag.

"Tell us how she becomes young again," pressed Lizzie.

Grandpa smiled at her. "When the last of the snows have gone, the Blue Hag raises her staff aloft and sings out a long note that carries from one hill to the next. When the sound dies away, she is transformed, and walks off the hill a beautiful young woman. Then Spring has returned. It's the turning of the year – the season wheel has moved on." He paused. "We'll catch up with her tomorrow."

The next morning was dismal and damp, which set the pattern for the day. The Blue Hag showed no sign of coming out, and reluctantly Grandpa suggested that they would be as well to return to Edinburgh. Packing their things, they headed back for the low road.

Find out more about the magyckal Shian world
and keep up-to-date with news of the second and third
books in the trilogy!

www.shianquest.com

You can also find us on Facebook!